Heat on the Street

By Josh Anderson

Scobre Press Corporation
2255 Calle Clara
La Jolla, CA 92307

First Scobre edition published 2009.
Edited by Charlotte Graeber   .
Illustrated by Bill Wiist
Cover Design by Michael Lynch

ISBN (10) #1-934713-94-5
ISBN (13) #978-1-934713-94-5

HOME RUN EDITION

CHAPTER ONE

ON THE ROOFTOPS

"You got an anonymous tip your first week on the job?" asked Tim O'Rourke from the driver's seat of his unmarked Ford Taurus. "You have no idea how unusual that is, Rookie."

I didn't know who had sent the email. It alerted me to the sound of gunshots at the abandoned Skypoint Theater. Still, I wasn't about to ignore it—even if my new partner was sure this tip would lead us nowhere.

"Well, I like being unusual," I replied. "It keeps things interesting. Doesn't it, Timmy?" I smiled sarcastically at my new partner. The time was 7:23 a.m.

The car came to a shrieking stop. Tim's eyes pointed at me like daggers. "If you call me Timmy again, you and I will have a problem."

It was only my third day. But I could tell my new partner wasn't a big fan of mine. My name's Bobby Cortez, and I like to do things my way. Tim, on the other hand, was an accomplished agent. He'd been with the FBI for more than 20 years. While I had plenty to learn from him, I wasn't about to kiss up to him. "I didn't mean to get you riled up, Tim," I said.

Tim and I were as different as partners could be. He was "by the book" all the way. His father and both of his grandfathers had been policemen. He'd been raised with a strict image of how a lawman was supposed to act. A smart-mouthed rookie like me, who liked to do things by the seat of his pants, got under Tim's skin in a big way.

Those first few days, Tim never passed up the chance to remind me that there was a right way to practice law enforcement—and a wrong way. Most of our conversations started out with Tim saying something like, "Rookies don't know squat."

Because I didn't take the usual path to the FBI, Tim felt even less confident about working with me. Most agents work in their local police departments or as lawyers before applying to the Bureau. Not me—I was a former high school teacher and track coach in Buffalo, New York.

As a teacher, I had my own style, too. That's one of the things that made me good at the job. I can no longer influence the lives of New York's best minds from inside the classroom. But as an FBI special agent, I can try to keep them safe outside of it. Of course, I plan on doing it my way.

We exited Tim's car, and I led the way up to the

abandoned Skypoint Theater in Brooklyn. The place was dark and deserted. We moved carefully through a small hole in the wooden boards covering the front of the building. This was the heart of gang territory, so we were ready to draw our weapons at any moment.

Tim shook his head as we ducked inside. "What a burnout this old place is," he said.

"Wasn't always," I whispered.

"What's that?" Tim asked.

"Nothing," I said. "My tip said last night's gunshots came from upstairs."

FBI agents are almost never the first on the scene of a crime. Federal agents like us generally come on board after "unis"—regular cops who wear standard uniforms—have already taken stock of a crime scene.

As we moved slowly in the dark, we heard footsteps above us. "Identify yourself," Tim yelled. There was no response. Then we heard some shuffling, followed by running. "FBI, stay where you are!" he called out.

Without waiting for my partner, I turned right and bolted up the stairs.

"Hang on, Cortez!" Tim yelled in an annoyed voice.

I was long gone, racing after the footsteps I had heard. They stopped suddenly when I reached the second floor. It was pitch-black, except for a small light coming from the projector room. I headed in with my heart racing and my finger on the trigger of my Glock-22. I was ready to fire if my life was in danger—although I hoped I wouldn't have to.

I noticed a strong smell of paint in the air. This was strange, because it was obvious no one had worried about the walls in here for a long time. I crept toward an open door, which led to a small deck outside. I was trying to avoid the three projector tables in front of me. But then, I nearly tripped and fell flat on my face.

When I looked down, I noticed a body lying on the ground in front of me. The few strands of light pouring in revealed a puddle of blood. The man was lying in the middle of it. My heart nearly stopped. I had never been so close to a dead person.

"Hello?" I asked, trying to confirm what I already assumed. There was no answer. I felt behind his ear to check for a pulse. There was none. The body was cold and stiff, which meant it had been there a while. The dead man's shirt was covered with blood from two gunshot wounds. His neck was cut, too. It was a terrible scene.

"Cortez, where are you?" Tim yelled from downstairs.

I shouted down, "We got a body up here."

Just then, I heard a noise coming from the other side of the open door. Someone was definitely out there. Springing to my feet, I headed for the door. I exited onto a small outdoor deck.

I noticed a ladder going up to the roof of the theater

and quickly stepped onto it. I hustled up to the rooftop.

Once up there, I saw a man in a white hoodie standing about 50 feet away from me. He was holding a can of spray paint. I moved slowly across the roof and made eye contact with him. "I didn't do it," he yelled.

I took a deep breath and dug my fingernails into my palms.

"I believe you," I yelled back, reaching slowly for my gun. "Come with me and let's talk about it."

It's never that easy, though. A second later, the guy took off running. I started after him toward the other end of the rooftop. There was another, shorter building next door. I walked toward him, waiting for him to fall to his knees so I could take him in.

"You got nowhere to go!" I screamed. I raised my gun and shouted, "Put your hands over your head and—" Right in the middle of this sentence, I watched him take off like a bird. He leapt over the 5-foot gap between buildings and skidded onto the next rooftop. I couldn't believe he'd tried the jump, or that he'd made it. Now, I had a decision to make: to jump or not to jump?

There was no time to think. I moved to the ledge and saw the man run across the next rooftop and head for the other end. Nobody outruns Bobby Cortez, I thought. I couldn't let this guy get away.

I took a long and deep breath. Without another thought, I sprinted toward the ledge...

It felt like I hung in the air forever. I flew toward the other rooftop and landed with my hands behind me like a long jumper.

Standing up quickly, I started running again. The man in the hoodie had almost reached the other side of the rooftop. Without stopping, he turned back to see if he had lost me. When he saw that I was still after him, he leapt to the next rooftop. The gap was even larger than the last one. I saw the can of spray paint fall from his pocket into a dumpster in the alley below.

I was sure there was nowhere for him to go, except the street, three stories down. The next rooftop over was way too far for him to jump to. But to arrest him, I'd still have to make this last jump myself.

I started sprinting toward the ledge, not sure I would make it. The man in the hoodie reached the other end of the roof just as I took off. He was running out of options and knew it. I hung in the air again for what felt like an hour, reaching my arms toward the next building…

I made it—sort of. My upper half landed softly. But my legs crashed into the front of the building with a painful thud.

I pulled myself up and walked toward the mysterious man. I was still trying to catch my breath. He was standing at the other end of the roof. "It's over," I said, flashing my badge. "Put your hands in the air."

He turned away from me and looked down at the

street below. I noticed an orange handkerchief hanging from his back pocket. He's a Tigre, I thought, recognizing that bandana instantly. He turned back toward me, reached into his other pocket, and pulled out a knife.

I took a step back, pulling my gun from its holster. At that moment, I started to realize that this was more of a boy than a man. He was 17, maybe younger. His hands and neck were covered in gang tattoos. His skin was olive like my own. It looked to me like we shared a Puerto Rican heritage.

"Don't do this," I said, pointing the gun at him. "Put the knife down!"

I released the safety on my gun. We each stood for a moment without moving. Would I shoot him? I wondered. I was ready to do what I needed to. Or, at least I thought I was.

"¿Por qué mataste a ese hombre?" I spoke to him in Spanish. I was asking him why he'd killed the man in the projector room.

The kid in the hoodie looked confused. "I speak English. And I told you, I didn't kill nobody!"

"Then put down the knife," I said. "And let's talk about it."

A sense of relief rushed over me as I watched him toss the knife onto the roof. I'd almost broken the skin of my right hand by digging my fingernails into my palm. This was a nervous habit I'd had since childhood.

Sighing loudly, I put my gun back into its holster. "Good decision," I said. But before I could take another step, he leapt off the rooftop to the street below. It must have been a 30-foot drop.

I hurried toward the ledge and watched his arms flail in the air and his legs run in place. I thought there was no way he'd make the jump without a major injury. But I saw him land, pause for a moment, then stand up and run away with a slight limp. Then he disappeared from my view.

I considered trying the jump myself. But every second I stood there thinking about it, my chances of catching him dwindled. Just then, I heard Tim's loud voice call to me from three rooftops away. "You might as well jump, Rook, because I'm gonna knock you out for this. Meet me back at my car!" he shouted. "And take the stairs or I'll arrest you."

"Arrest me for what?" I asked.

"Stupidity," he replied.

I knew I'd broken quite a few rules by leaving Tim alone and risking my life on these rooftops. Now I'd have to face the wrath of my angry partner, and our boss, the director.

Yes, what I did seemed totally reckless. But the truth was, I knew this place very well. I'd been in that theater a hundred times as a kid. The Skypoint neighborhood of Brooklyn had been my home for the first 14 years of my life.

I joined Tim downstairs a short time later. "What took you so long?" asked Tim.

"I was dumpster diving," I told him. I held up the can of spray paint that the guy in the hoodie had dropped. "Let's go take a better look at the crime scene."

"No," Tim said. "That's what I was doing while you were playing Spiderman up there. I got all the info we need already."

"Listen, Tim, I know I went too far, but I had to try to—" I started to say.

"It was a dumb move—and you're lucky you didn't end up dead." Tim's intensity turned softer. "You've got heart, kid. The way you chased that guy and jumped those rooftops was impressive. Stupid and dangerous, but impressive," he said.

"Thanks, I guess," I said as I got into the car.

Tim turned to me with a serious expression. "You know where my grandfather is buried?" he asked.

"What?" I had no idea where he was going with this.

"He's buried to the left of my grandmother, and to the right of his partner," Tim said. "They patrolled together for 24 years."

Tim got very close to my face. "You don't leave your partner alone—ever. My partner of 21 years retired last month—which is why we're together now. And in 21 years he never left me like that. You do something like that again, I'll eat you for lunch," he said.

"All right," I said. "I'm sorry. But why can't I go look at the crime scene?"

"'Cause I've already called in the unis. They'll have a photographer in there soon," Tim said. "You can see the pictures later. Believe me, Rookie, you're not gonna catch anything I didn't." I couldn't believe that Tim wasn't even going to let me have a look at the crime scene. Tim saw my frustrated expression and continued lecturing me. "You're in the heart of gang country. You're chasing some hoodlum alone across a bunch of old rooftops that he knows like the back of his hand. That's a good way to end up dead."

I silently slunk back into my seat as Tim drove away. There was a lot that my partner didn't know about me. I also knew those rooftops—all too well.

CHAPTER TWO

MEETING WITH THE DIRECTOR

The next day, Tim and I sat in the waiting room at the office of New York's FBI director, Emmett McDowell. I hadn't seen McDowell since my final interview before I headed to the FBI Academy in Quantico, Virginia.

The first time I laid eyes on him, it was hard to take him seriously. He had shoulder-length gray hair that he wore in a ponytail. He also made odd fashion choices. Still, it didn't take long to learn that appearances could be deceiving. I'd never met someone who commanded so much respect with just his eyes.

McDowell had suffered the ultimate loss during the terrorist attacks of September 11, 2001. That day, he learned that his son, a promising young agent, had been killed during rescue attempts when the North Tower collapsed.

Six months ago, during my final interview, Mc-Dowell had asked me: "Are you ready, Mr. Cortez, to be the one running toward danger, even as others are running away?"

I nodded. "I am ready, sir."

"Good," he told me, "because if you're not, the Academy will eat you alive."

McDowell had been right. My four and a half months at the FBI Academy were probably the most difficult of my entire life. Looking back, they were also the most exciting. The daily exercise routines put me in the best shape of my life. And the training exercises taught me all sorts of martial arts and weapons training. By the end of my 20 weeks, I knew I could handle whatever the streets had in store for me.

Still, every trainee was under tremendous pressure. I made it through, but I watched some other strong men and women fall apart and flunk out.

Now, I was sitting in McDowell's waiting room the morning after the events at the Skypoint Theater. I had no idea what to expect. "Did you tell McDowell I left you alone in the theater? Is that why we're here?" I anxiously whispered over to Tim.

He looked at me like I had three heads. "One of my uncles was partners with a guy for about half his time on the force in Minnesota," Tim said, beginning one of his long stories. "He hated him. He used to drink on the job, and even take a bribe now and then. My uncle used to complain about this guy all the time when I was a kid."

My eyes started to glaze over again. I'd lost track of how many of Tim's relatives had been police officers. "And your point is?" I asked.

"My uncle probably could've gotten this guy thrown off the force about five different times. But he didn't—because you don't rat on your partner!" Tim said.

"Okay, I get it," I said. "Thanks." I was glad to hear that Tim hadn't shared my mistake with McDowell. "I got your back, too, Tim. I mean, if we ever—"

In the middle of my sentence, McDowell's assistant told us he was ready, so we headed in. He was wearing a striped red jacket with a bright yellow tie. Sitting on his desk was the can of spray paint that I'd recovered from the dumpster.

We sat waiting for almost a minute before the director spoke. I started to get concerned that we were in big trouble.

"Agent O'Rourke?" McDowell asked coldly.

"Yes, sir?" Tim answered.

McDowell held up the can of spray paint. "What is this?"

Hesitantly, Tim answered, "A can of spray paint, sir. We recovered it from the suspect who got away from us in Skypoint."

"What were you two doing in Brooklyn," the director asked, "when all of your cases are in Manhattan and the Bronx?"

I couldn't let Tim take the blame just because he was the senior agent on the team. "It's my fault," I said. "I received a tip about gunshots, sir."

"Was I speaking to you, Agent Cortez?" McDowell scowled at me.

My first week on the job, and I had gotten myself in big trouble already. "I read the report you prepared, Agent O'Rourke. Cortez over here dancing on rooftops like he's on the playground is definitely not FBI protocol. And you," he pointed at Tim. "You almost let the rookie get killed in his first week. You know better than that."

I couldn't believe he was blaming Tim for this. He had nothing to do with my choice to go after the guy on the rooftops. I started to protest again. "Sir, can I just say something—?" Before I finished my sentence, McDowell turned his glare at me again. I could practically see the smoke coming out of his ears.

Then he looked over at Tim. "Give me a moment alone with Cortez, please." McDowell walked Tim out of the room. He put his hand on Tim's shoulder and spoke firmly, "You're one of the best agents I've got, O'Rourke. But you better put a leash on this puppy—and quickly. His mistakes are your mistakes."

I avoided Tim's eyes as he left the room. I felt ashamed and embarrassed. Now, left alone with McDowell, I shrunk into my chair, waiting to get chewed out.

"Let me make something crystal clear, Cortez: If

you head off on a reckless chase along some rooftops in gangland ever again, you will not be an FBI agent anymore," McDowell said. "Is that understood?"

"Yes, sir," I said.

"We hire 750 agents a year. There's a fair share who don't make it through the two-year probation period. Some get fired. Some don't have the stomach for it. And a few of them—some who do stupid things like you did—get killed."

While I didn't like it, I knew McDowell was right. I had to prove to McDowell—and to myself—that I'd come a long way from the reckless Bobby Cortez of my youth.

I looked straight into McDowell's eyes and said, "It won't happen again."

"It had better not," he said. "Now, there's something else."

"Is it the can of spray paint, sir? Was there a DNA match to the kid on the rooftop?" I asked.

McDowell cracked a smile. "This is not an episode of 'CSI,' Cortez."

McDowell went on to describe CODIS for me. CODIS is the database the FBI uses to match DNA from a crime scene to their database of suspects.

I rubbed my eyes to make sure they didn't permanently glaze over. After all, I had just spent four months studying CODIS at the Academy. I wouldn't need a refresher course anytime soon.

"Even though we're the FBI," he continued, "we rely on good, old-fashioned police work more than high-tech equipment. With a little elbow grease, you'll have plenty of info on this case long before a CODIS scan could tell you anything."

I was shocked. "So, we're going to be able to work this case?" I'd assumed that local police would take over.

"For now, you two can continue what you started," McDowell said. He held up the can of spray paint and pointed to some scribbles on it. It read "Mordida feroz." I recognized the Spanish words instantly. "You know what these words mean, don't you?"

I couldn't believe that I hadn't noticed this when I recovered the can. "That's the Tigres' tag," I said.

McDowell nodded.

I knew the FBI had looked into my background when I applied to become an agent. But, deep down, I'd hoped that there were some things that would stay in the past. For me, my time with the Tigres was one of them.

"We've got a bad situation in Brooklyn," McDowell said. "Gangs are taking over the streets. The Skypoint neighborhood is becoming the center of it. The Tigres gang were small-time thugs when you were growing up. Now they've got a big industry of drugs and violence in Brooklyn. And when you've got a gang trying to prove they're big time, bodies start piling up."

I nodded. Federal agents generally left neighborhood violence and drugs to the local cops. I was surprised to hear that the Tigres had gotten dangerous enough to get onto the FBI's radar screen.

"I've been asked to set my sights on curbing gang violence in the city," McDowell continued. "I need someone out there who knows the streets inside and out. Someone who knows that world personally."

My mind started to wander backward to things and people I hadn't thought much about in years. "I'll do my best, but I haven't known that world in a long time, sir."

"You sure knew your way around that movie theater in the dark, and across those rooftops." McDowell leaned forward and asked, "Can you spend some time in that world again—for the Bureau?"

I nodded my head. "That's why I joined, sir."

"Good," McDowell said, pressing the button on his intercom. "Send O'Rourke back in."

Moments later, Tim walked into the office and McDowell handed him a folder. "Your case is in here. I want the body you two found today to be the last person to die at the hands of the Tigres."

Tim looked over at me with a smile. He was clearly excited that we had been assigned this case.

"Cortez, keep in mind that Agent O'Rourke is in charge. Am I clear?" McDowell asked.

"Yes, sir," I answered as Tim flipped through a stack

of photos in the folder.

When I caught a glimpse of one of the photos, I nearly jumped backward in shock. Then I took the photo and stared closely at it. I turned back to McDowell, who shot me a knowing look. "The man you see in that photo is the head of the Tigres. He's connected, if not directly responsible, for the dead body you found yesterday," McDowell informed us.

At that moment, the world seemed to be spinning. I stared at the face in the photograph—a face from my past that I knew very well. Everything else fell out of my mind. My thoughts went back 14 years, to another place and another time...

CHAPTER THREE

UP, UP AND AWAY

A trip to Coney Island with my two best friends, Jorge Orosco and Raffy Perez, turned out to be one of the more memorable days of my youth. It was the summer before high school started—when life was carefree and fun.

We were 13 years old and Brooklyn was our entire world. It was rare that we even left Skypoint, the neighborhood where we'd all spent nearly our entire lives.

Coney Island was a neighborhood located right on the beach, on the southern tip of Brooklyn. Whether you were looking for the world's best hot dog, fun in the ocean, or the scariest roller coaster, Coney Island was the place.

That day, we were headed to Astroland Park. It was home of the Cyclone, a famous, old wooden roller coaster with a ridiculous free-fall drop.

Hopping off the bus, Jorge led the way. He was the oldest and biggest of the three of us. No one except Raffy or I would have the nerve to make fun of him for it, but he would skip like a girl when he got excited. Now, he was racing across Surf Avenue toward Astroland. Raffy and I did our best not to laugh at Jorge as he skipped toward the ticket booth.

Jorge could eat twice as much as either Raffy or I. On the bus ride over, we dared him to eat 10 hot dogs before we went home that night. He said he'd eat 20 if Raffy and I were paying. We agreed, because the little bit of pocket money we had was always shared among all of us anyway.

Raffy was the brains of our trio—book smart, but frail and clumsy. We would joke that the reason he was always tripping was that his brain was too heavy for his body. He was the only one of us who had two parents at home. They were really strict with him, and he was always worried about getting grounded. There wasn't a more loyal friend than skinny Raffy. If I was upset, Raffy was the first one I'd go to—after my dad.

Before we reached the ticket booth, we stopped by a hot dog stand. Each of us finished three dogs. We didn't make Jorge go through with his 20 hot dog promise because we wanted to save money for the rides. Plus, we didn't want to smell his farts for the rest of the afternoon.

A few minutes later, we arrived at the ticket booth for the Cyclone. Once there, we experienced a huge disappointment. We only had enough money left over for one of us to ride. None of us had ever been on a roller coaster before. We walked away from the ticket booth totally upset.

"Let's watch everyone else ride," Jorge suggested. "Maybe somebody will feel bad for us and give us a ticket."

We watched the ride in silence for a few minutes from right near the operation center. Unfortunately, nobody gave us a ticket. A few feet away, the ride operator controlled the entire coaster with one big red lever.

Jorge suggested we try to sneak on. But Raffy would never try something like that—not without a super-smart plan.

"Let's go to the beach for a while," I said. "I've got an idea that might work, but we'll have to wait."

Raffy and Jorge followed me toward the park exit and up to the famous Coney Island boardwalk. We spent the rest of the day swimming in the ocean, eating more hot dogs, and trying to get the attention of girls who walked by.

Once the night came, we headed back into Astroland Park. I told the guys about my plan: We would find a good place to hide and wait for the park to close—then ride the Cyclone after everyone had left. I had watched the operator for long enough so that I pretty much knew how the Cyclone worked.

Within a few minutes, Jorge found the perfect hiding spot. In a dark corner, we saw a tarp wrapped around a huge plastic tube. It looked like a giant roll of paper towels lying on its side. We squeezed in like sardines, sitting side by side. Nobody could see us. Then we waited—and waited some more—for Astroland Park to shut its doors for the night. The plan was in motion.

About two hours later we came out from under the tarp. We were the only ones in the entire park. We stood in front of the Cyclone and stared at it. I hopped over the gate and into the ride operator's booth. Jorge skipped over to the roller coaster and took a seat in the first car, and Raffy got in next to him. "Let's go already!" Jorge yelled with a smile.

"You sure you know how to work this thing?" Raffy shouted over to me.

I grabbed the huge red lever. "We'll see right now," I said, pulling it to my left and expecting the ride to begin. But nothing happened. "Uh-oh," I said, motioning for Jorge to come over.

"I ain't leaving here without taking a ride," he complained as he walked over, joining me in the operator's booth.

Next to the lever, there was a metal box with a lock on it that looked like it might hide a switch to turn the ride on. Jorge pulled out a small knife, which he kept on his keychain. He quickly pried the box open, breaking the lock. My heart skipped and my eyes met with Raffy's for a moment. We both quickly looked away. The two of us knew that what we were doing was wrong. But after waiting for almost 10 hours, we simply had to ride.

"Let's do this," Jorge said as he skipped toward the coaster, joining Raffy again in the front car.

I flipped one of the two switches and heard the power churn up. Next, the lever in front of me started to vibrate. "Here goes nothing," I yelled.

I pulled the red lever to my left and watched as the roller coaster cars started moving slowly forward. I raced from the operator's booth to the ride entrance.

"Hurry up," Raffy yelled as they moved toward the first huge drop.

I raced up the ramp and practically dove into the last car in the chain, just in time. Jorge and Raffy looked back at me from the first car, smiling and laughing. I stuffed my Mets cap under my legs and pulled the safety bar over them.

As we started rising, I had a big lump in my throat. Just outside the park, past the boardwalk and the beach, I could see the Atlantic Ocean. Unfortunately, I also saw a police car with its lights on parked just outside the park. It made me wish for a second that I was anywhere but here. But, looking up at my two best friends, laughing and screaming, I felt safe—for the moment.

As we reached the very top, I watched Jorge and Raffy disappear as they sank over the edge. I heard their happy screams and took a deep breath as my car reached the top.

The way down started slowly. But as the train sped up, I held on to the safety bar for dear life with one hand. I dug my fingernails into my palm with the other. Before I could catch my breath, we were racing toward another climb.

Jorge looked back at me, laughing. Raffy, on the other hand, looked paralyzed with fear. Still, I saw a hint of a smile when he turned his head. As for me, I just couldn't stop laughing.

A minute or two later, the Cyclone cars pulled back to the entrance, but the ride didn't slow down. We raced right through. We were slowly climbing up to the first steep drop again.

I hadn't thought about how we'd stop the ride to get off. When I'd watched the operator earlier, he had to pull the lever to slow the ride at the end.

My brain had never felt more scrambled. We rode the Cyclone 12 times before Raffy yelled that he felt sick and demanded that we stop.

"One of us is gonna have to jump next time," I yelled on the way up to the top on our 13th ride.

"Not me," Raffy screamed out.

"Not it!" Jorge yelled.

"Fine, I'll do it," I said. "You guys are such wimps."

As we pulled toward the end of the ride, I shimmied up the guard bar across my lap. I stood up and grabbed onto the side of my car. I put one foot up and got ready to jump. Then I lifted my other foot up and jumped onto the wooden slats at the ride's entrance. Hitting the ground hard, I rolled a few feet before I stopped. By the time I got up and reached the operator's booth, Jorge and Raffy were most of the way up to the first drop.

The next cycle around, I waited until just the right time. Then I eased back on the lever and brought the ride to a not-so-smooth stop. As Raffy and Jorge walked off, I switched the Cyclone off. A second later, I was shocked to hear clapping.

The three of us froze and looked over at two police officers walking toward us. "I was wondering how you idiots were going to stop the ride," one of them shouted, "cuz we sure weren't gonna stop it for you."

The three of us moved closer together as the cops approached. We could see their car parked right outside the park entrance. They'd left the gate to the park open behind them.

"You boys ever heard of trespassing?" the other cop asked, holding up a pair of handcuffs.

Raffy lowered his voice to a whisper so only Jorge and I could hear. "Get ready to run."

Just then, Raffy hunched over, grabbing his stomach. "I feel sick," he said.

Both cops bent down toward Raffy. "You all right, kid?" one of them asked.

"I don't know," Raffy said, taking a couple of steps forward. "It hurts. I'm gonna puke." The cops took a few steps back so as to not get vomited on.

A moment later, he started running. "C'mon," he shouted. "The bus is coming!"

Jorge and I exchanged a look of surprise and then took off behind Raffy as fast as we could. The two officers didn't react in time to grab us.

We didn't look back to see if they were chasing us until we were safely on the bus. It left the moment we stepped on it. The cops were standing by their car, shaking their heads. They'd decided that catching a bunch of kids wasn't worth chasing the bus down.

Jorge was lying flat on his back across from us, moaning. "Those hot dogs are sitting in my stomach like bricks," he said. "I never ran so fast in my life!"

I turned to Raffy, who had a look of quiet satisfaction on his face. "Where'd that come from?" I asked him. "You're usually scared to death of the police."

"No, I'm scared to death of my parents," he said. "If I'd left it to you two morons, we'd have spent the night in jail." We all started laughing.

That entire summer was just like that night: three 13-year-old friends finding every possible harmless way to have fun. Unfortunately, nothing ever stays the same.

CHAPTER FOUR

MAMACITA'S

Ten months after that day on the Cyclone, summer vacation was right around the corner again. We were just finishing our freshman year of high school, and it seemed like things were changing.

Heading up Avenue M one day in Skypoint, we were having one of our most common debates. "Raffy, you may do well in school, but you're the stupidest person I've ever met," Jorge said. "You're definitely the only kid in Brooklyn who doesn't like pizza—probably the only kid in all of New York."

"He may be stupid. But at least he knows that Mario's beats the crap out of Original Pizza any day," I said.

"You're crazy," Jorge said. "A slice at Mario's is 50 cents more and only has half as much cheese. Even Royal Pizza is better than Mario's."

We turned down East 93rd Street and headed toward Avenue L, the most action-packed street in Skypoint. The three of us would usually stay away when it was at its busiest, though. That's because hanging out there often meant getting hassled by some of the local thugs. They would steal your money or take your backpack if they knew you weren't in a gang.

During this past year, though, things had changed for us on The L. Jorge had made friends with some kids in the Tigres—the toughest gang in Skypoint. Anytime a gang member approached us now, they would give Jorge a fist bump. And they pretty much left Raffy and me alone.

Just before we turned onto Avenue L, in front of Mamacita's bodega, Jorge asked, "You guys want to have some fun?"

"What kind of fun?" Raffy asked, not too sure of Jorge's idea of fun lately.

"You know how I chill with some of the Tigres, right?" Jorge asked.

I nodded, signaling him to go on.

"Well, I'm sure you've both heard me talking about getting respect, too. I mean, life is all about earning respect, right?"

Raffy and I nodded our heads.

"Anyway," Jorge continued, "the Tigres told me I'd get mad respect if I stole some stuff from Mamacita's and brought it back to the crib where they all hang out."

"What kind of stuff do you want to steal?" I asked.

"Candy and some drinks is all," Jorge said.

"Mamacita won't even miss it. I'll take care of everything. You two just distract whoever's working. I'll do the rest."

I knew stealing was wrong, but this sounded like an exciting adventure. Being in a gang was something I had never been interested in. But it seemed cool that all of these older kids were friendly to Jorge now. To be honest, I was kind of jealous.

"I'm in," I said, pretending to feel confident.

Raffy looked very nervous. "I don't know, Jorge."

"Man, I didn't think we were walking around Skypoint with such a chicken," Jorge said.

There wasn't much worse than being called a chicken when you were 14 years old. "What if I'm the lookout?" Raffy asked, although I could tell his heart wasn't in it.

Jorge shook his head. "Just go home. We don't need a lookout. Let's go, Bobby."

"I'll keep watch and tell you if I see any cops," Raffy called out after us.

"Just go! You'd never get any respect from the Tigres anyway," Jorge said.

I watched Raffy's face fall. He was the smartest kid in our whole school and had a different way of thinking. Sometimes it meant that kids would be mean to him. Throughout our lives, Jorge and I had always made a point to stick up for Raffy. Lately, though, Jorge seemed to treat Raffy the same way a lot of other kids did.

As we walked toward Mamacita's, I said to Jorge, "You shouldn't be so cold to Raffy." Jorge blew me off and changed the subject. He started explaining what he wanted me to do once we got into the store.

The bell on the door rang as we entered Mamacita's. The owner's son, Alfred, was there. He was in his 20s and we didn't know him well. He was huge and had been a football player at Skypoint High School. He wasn't known for being a genius, though. People joked that he'd taken one too many hits on the football field.

Mamacita's was small. Alfred sat behind the counter, reading the sports page of the newspaper. He greeted us with a friendly "hola" when we entered.

I headed toward the back. Jorge went over to the candy, located on a rack right below the cash register. I was scared because I had never stolen anything before. From the corner of my eye, I could see Jorge pretending to decide what kind of candy he wanted. He looked at me and opened his eyes wide, waiting for me to do something.

Lately, I felt like I had to impress Jorge. I looked around and then stopped at the beverage coolers. "Hey," I yelled up to Alfred, trying to think quickly.

"What's up?" Alfred yelled back.

"I don't see any cream soda."

"Cream soda? I don't remember ever carrying cream soda," Alfred said.

"I buy it here all the time. Ask Mamacita," I said.

"She ain't here right now," Alfred said. "You sure you buy it here?"

"Yeah, like once a week. My grandma drinks a cream soda before bed every night, or she can't sleep," I said, even though both of my grandmothers lived in Puerto Rico. They probably had never even tasted cream soda.

"All right, let me check." I smiled to myself. Alfred may have been older, but he couldn't match wits with me.

He left the register and went into the stockroom in back. I knew we didn't have a lot of time.

As soon as he disappeared into the back, I gave a nod to Jorge. Then I turned my back to Jorge so I could keep a lookout for Alfred. I heard Jorge rustling a bit around the counter.

Maybe I should've felt bad about what we were doing, but I didn't. The rush that came with the fear of getting caught was new and exciting. "Hurry up," I said to Jorge, turning around. To my surprise, Jorge was behind the counter now. "What are you doing, stupid?" I asked him.

Jorge turned a cold stare in my direction. "Don't call me stupid, Bobby. I know we're boys, but if you show me disrespect, I'll mess you up."

I'm sure my face couldn't hide my shock. Jorge had never spoken to me that way—not in the 10 years we'd been friends. I didn't say anything back. But at that moment, I desperately wanted to leave the store.

31

I watched as Jorge, still behind the counter, started grabbing packs of cigarettes. He was stuffing them into his book bag. I wanted to ask him, "Who are you and what did you do with my friend?" But I was too scared.

All of a sudden, Alfred popped out from the back and looked right at me, somehow not noticing Jorge. "No cream soda back there. Everything we got is in here," he said, pointing to the refrigerator. He started to move toward the counter. "Sorry kid, maybe your grandma will settle for a root beer."

"Uh," I muttered, unsure of what to say.

Alfred looked down at me and raised an eyebrow. I could tell that he was beginning to catch on that something was up. Just then, Alfred looked up toward the front of the store. I could see the confusion on his face melt away, quickly turning to anger. "Wait!" he screamed. "Get back here!"

I heard the bell on the door ring and knew Jorge was long gone. Alfred looked down at me with rage in his eyes. "You set me up," he yelled, reaching out to grab my arm. I spun away, then sprinted down the center aisle of the store.

I reached the front door of Mamacita's and felt Alfred close on my heels. On my right was a display rack with Coke cans stacked on it. I threw the display down behind me to slow him down. Alfred halted as dozens of cans came crashing to the ground between me and him. I pushed my way out the front door without looking back.

Jorge was half a block up Avenue L by the time I got out of the store. He didn't look like he was waiting for me. But there was one thing that would never change. I was the fastest kid in the neighborhood. "Bobby Bullet" was my nickname.

I headed after Jorge. Looking over my shoulder, I saw Alfred locking the door to Mamacita's so he could chase after us. I started to catch up to Jorge with Alfred a safe distance behind us. Then I looked back and noticed that Raffy was running behind me as well. He was about 20 yards ahead of Alfred. I couldn't just leave him, so I slowed down to give him a chance to catch up.

We weaved through the crowd outside the Skypoint Theater together. "What are you still doing here?" I asked as we ran down the street.

Raffy could barely get a word out while he ran. "Keeping watch," he said.

We saw Jorge turn onto East 96th Street and we followed him. Alfred was gaining on us. Raffy was like a 50-pound weight on my back. "Let's go, Raffy," I yelled. "Run faster!"

I looked toward the busy block ahead. This was our best chance to get lost in the crowd and get away from Alfred. Just then, I heard a smack next to me. I looked to my left and saw Raffy in a heap on the ground. He'd tripped and was holding his knee. His pants had ripped and he was bleeding.

I stopped and looked down at him—and then up at Alfred, who was quickly gaining on us. I picked up Raffy by the armpits. "C'mon Raf, you're going to get all of us in big trouble. Let's go," I said.

We sprinted together toward the end of the block, and quickly made a right onto East 96th. Just as we turned the corner, I heard a "psssst" coming from the direction of one of the houses on the block.

I noticed the lid on a garbage pail shaking. Then I saw Jorge's head pop up. "Hide in these," he said, pointing to a group of empty pails next to his.

I raced to one and hopped in. I tried not to breathe in the funky smell, but that was impossible. Raffy jumped into the pail beside me. Even though the pails were empty, they were old and nasty. My pail smelled like a mixture of pee, rotten fruit and old cheese.

Peeking out from under the garbage pail cover, I watched Alfred run past us up the street. He screamed out into the street, "I'm calling the police! You'll all go to jail for this!"

We had to wait 15 minutes for Alfred to finally give up and head back to the store. Finally, when the coast was clear, we climbed out. As soon as Raffy got out, I saw that his knee was bleeding pretty badly. "How am I gonna explain this to my mom?" he asked.

Jorge said, "You lie to her, that's how. You don't tell

her about what we did. You got it?"

Raffy looked at Jorge, more disappointed than scared. "Of course not. Why would I do that?"

"Cuz sometimes you act like a whiny punk! You just better not tell her. Or you're gonna have a problem with me and the Tigres," Jorge said, heading down the street. He turned to me, holding up his book bag. "I gotta drop this off. You coming?"

I wanted to stand up for Raffy. I wanted to tell him that there would be more times for the three of us to hang out, like the night on the Cyclone. But at that moment, I knew things had changed—maybe permanently. I turned my back on Raffy and headed off in the other direction with Jorge.

"Where are we going?" I asked him, once Raffy was out of sight.

"I got a good place for us to hide," he said.

CHAPTER FIVE

THE CRIB

It took us about 10 minutes to get to the rundown apartment building. The place was located on East 105th Street, which wasn't the best part of town. I must've looked over my shoulder a hundred times on the way there.

Jorge laughed at me for looking so nervous. Surprisingly, he didn't look concerned at all. I was even more shocked when my best friend lit up a cigarette. I had never seen him smoke before. "So, what is this place?" I asked Jorge as we approached the entrance to the building.

"This is where the Tigres chill," he said. "They call it 'The Crib.'"

I smiled nervously. "The Tigres?" I asked. "I don't know any of those guys. I'm not sure if they'll like that I'm—"

"You'll be safe here, Bobby. Because you do know one of the Tigres." I couldn't believe what Jorge was telling me: He was a Tigre, too. I didn't have much time to let it sink in before I was following him upstairs. "You sure they're not gonna care that I'm here?" I asked.

"Just be cool," Jorge said. We reached the doorway of apartment 403 and he knocked. I couldn't believe we were about to hang out with the Tigres.

"Who is it?" a voice asked from inside the apartment.

"Amaturo," Jorge answered.

The door opened just enough for Jorge to slide through. For a moment, I stood outside and hesitated. Jorge turned around and looked at me with cold eyes. "C'mon," he said.

I squeezed through the door and found myself standing in a dark, smoky living room. Rap music blasted as eight or nine guys and a few girls sat around on beat-up couches. Two skinny-looking thugs were playing video games. Another guy was drinking alcohol, and it seemed like everyone was smoking cigarettes.

One of the girls sat on the lap of one of the guys. They were kissing each other like there weren't other people in the room—only there were.

I'd never tried drinking or drugs, and hadn't really kissed a girl either. Seeing all these kids with no adults around, doing whatever they wanted, was something I had never been exposed to before. There was something pretty cool about it. Still, every eye in the room felt like it was on me. I'm not sure I had ever felt so uncomfortable.

Jorge looked at the Tigres on the couches. "Yo, this is Bobby. He's gonna chill here for a minute to stay away from the po-po," he said. I wondered if the other guys could tell that Jorge didn't always talk like that.

I looked up for a second and nodded to the group, hoping to look tough by not speaking.

Jorge started to introduce the Tigres. "This is Capone, and his girl Charisse," he said. Then he pointed to a really fat guy in a New York Jets jersey. "That's Big Rico, and that's Maria. And that's FDR."

FDR took a swig from his beer and looked up. "Stands for 'Free Dominican Republic,'" he said.

Suddenly, a voice came from the hallway. "Who the hell is this?"

"What's up, Guapo," Jorge said.

Everyone in the room turned toward Guapo, a man a few years older than the other Tigres. "Don't wassup me, son. Who is that?" Guapo asked again, pointing right at me with his cigarette.

Guapo wore a tank-top undershirt revealing the biggest tattoo-covered arms I'd ever seen. He walked toward me and fixed his cold eyes on Jorge. "Who is this kid?" he asked again. "He ain't supposed to be here, esse. Don't you know the rules?" Guapo smacked Jorge on the back of his head hard enough to knock him down.

I didn't have to look at Jorge to know how scared he was. "He's my friend. I thought it would be okay now that

I'm officially a Tigre," Jorge muttered.

"Well, you thought wrong," Guapo said, getting right in Jorge's face and slapping him again. When Jorge rose to his feet, Guapo pushed him hard against the door. "No outsiders allowed in The Crib! Now we got a situation." Guapo took a long drag off his cigarette and held it in his mouth as he exhaled. "Give me your hand," he said to Jorge.

"What?" Jorge asked.

Guapo grabbed Jorge's right hand, turning his palm upward. Then Guapo pulled the cigarette from his mouth and stubbed the lit end into Jorge's hand. "Follow the rules!"

Jorge squealed, his knees buckling from the pain. He slid down the wall and screamed for a full 10 seconds. Guapo let go of the butt and Jorge pulled it off his skin.

Guapo stepped away from Jorge and turned his angry eyes on me. "Who are you?"

I could barely get the words out as Guapo moved closer to me. "Bobby. I'm Jorge's friend. We thought it would be okay."

"Well, it's not," he said. "You know who we are?"

I nodded and dug my nails into my palms.

"So, how do I know you're not going to run tell Mommy or the police about where the Tigres hang out?"

I had to think quickly. Guapo looked like he would definitely hurt me if I gave the wrong answer. I wanted to show him that I was worthy of respect. "I don't have a mom anymore, and I don't talk to pigs," I said, using an insulting term for the police.

"Oh, is that right?" he asked, seeming a bit amused.

Jorge pulled a handful of cash out of his book bag. "He helped me steal this," Jorge mumbled. This got Guapo's attention. I was as surprised about the money as Guapo was. I had no idea Jorge had taken that cash from the register at Mamacita's.

Guapo took the money, and Jorge pulled some more out of the bag along with about 20 packs of cigarettes. Guapo took all the bills, counted them, rolled them into a tight wad, and then wrapped a rubber band around it. "Three-twenty here. Not bad. You helped him get this?" he asked me.

I didn't know what to say. If I had known Jorge was going to steal money from Mamacita's, I never would've gone along with him.

"It's okay, I ain't the cops," Guapo said, and then he started to laugh. The mood lightened and everyone else in the room laughed, too.

Guapo called over his shoulder, projecting his voice loudly, "'Zuma, come out here a sec."

I couldn't believe what was happening. Everyone in my neighborhood knew who Montezuma was. He was the head of the Tigres and a powerful presence in Skypoint. Montezuma was practically a celebrity around my 'hood.

Even if you were like me and hadn't met him, you'd heard stories about him.

A huge figure appeared in the doorway. While the rest of the Tigres were teenagers who looked more like boys, Montezuma was a grown man in his 20s. He commanded the respect of everyone in the room, and everything stopped when he entered.

Guapo showed him the roll of cash. "Amaturo brought this other kid here with him. They stole this cash. I don't wanna just let him go and next thing you know, we've got police banging down the door, you know?"

"Who are you?" Montezuma asked, stepping closer to me.

My mouth was so dry from being nervous that it was hard to even get my name out. "Bobby Cortez."

"You got a wallet?" he asked.

I took out my wallet, figuring he was going to take the $10 I had. Instead, he took my bus pass and examined the back with my name and address. Montezuma took the roll of cash from Guapo and stared into my eyes like he was testing me. I didn't dare look away. "You know who I am?" he asked.

I nodded as Montezuma leaned down, bringing his mouth to my ear. He took a deep breath inward and then spoke softly. "You don't smell like a rat. So go home. Don't come back here unless I personally ask you to. And keep your mouth shut. Otherwise, we'll take a trip to your house one night," he said, holding the bus pass and sliding it into his pocket.

Montezuma took a step back and held up the wad of cash. "This is a good start for you. I see some Tigre in you, Cortez. How do you feel about that?"

"Good," I said, smiling for the first time.

Adults always talked about how bad gangs were. But as I looked around the room, I started to think that maybe these guys weren't that bad. Except for Guapo, who I'd just seen burn Jorge. But Jorge had broken the rules, so I guess that kind of made sense, too. They lived by a code, and if you followed that code, it seemed like you would be okay. Besides, they definitely were having fun.

"Get out of here, Cortez," Montezuma said. I gave a quick nod to Jorge before I slid out the door. I ran down the long hallway and down the stairs of the apartment building.

I felt a great sense of relief when I left the building. But at the same time, part of me wished it were me, not Jorge, staying to hang out with the Tigres.

I raced home, afraid that the police might be looking for me. I thought about my dad and how upset he'd be if I got caught. He'd been a single father since my mother died more than 10 years ago. Dad had brought me to New York from Puerto Rico when I was 3. He worked construction during the day so he could support the two of us. He also did security work at a local bar at night to earn extra money for my college fund.

When he'd get home from the long nights, he'd always make the same joke. "Tonight was a good night, Roberto. I think I just paid for your freshman college English class," he'd say.

I had never stolen anything before. Now I'd helped Jorge steal more than $300 for the Tigres. Was I going to get caught and go to jail? Were my college dreams over? I'd definitely touched a few things in the store. What if there were fingerprints? I remembered learning in school that you could trace someone's DNA from a single hair. What if some of my hair was still in the store?

These questions raced through my brain. I became more and more convinced that I was going to jail for what I had done. I was also convinced that my father would never look at me the same.

When I arrived home, my worst fears seemed to be realized. An empty police car was parked right in front of the two-family house we lived in. There was no point in running. I crept up the stairs to our front door as quietly as I could. The last person I wanted to see right then was my father.

CHAPTER SIX

AN INVITATION

I looked through the front window of my house. I felt like all the air was suddenly sucked out of my lungs. That's because sitting at the kitchen table with my father was a uniformed police officer.

I turned the key to unlock our front door and hoped that my dreams weren't lost forever. I am going to be kicked off the track team. I can forget any scholarships. I can probably forget about college, too. I'll be lucky if my father ever talks to me again.

For a brief moment, I actually considered dropping my keys and running back to the Tigres' hideout. But my father noticed me peeking inside and waved for me to come in. It was weird because his face didn't look as angry as I thought it would.

I walked right over to my father and the police officer, a pretty African-American woman. I made eye contact with my father for a brief moment. Then I looked straight down, too ashamed to return his gaze.

I was determined not to rat on Jorge or give up any information on the Tigres. I decided that I wasn't going to offer any help at all, even if she was here to arrest me.

"Roberto, have a seat," my father said. He rarely used my full name, and I figured this meant I was in a lot of trouble. "I want you to meet Officer Patrice Kenyon."

My father shuffled uncomfortably in his chair. "Bobby, do you know why Officer Kenyon is here?"

I shook my head "no," not wanting to give them any evidence they didn't have already.

"Have you noticed anything different lately, Bobby?" my father asked.

I was surprised by the question. I looked up at my dad, then over at Officer Kenyon, who was smiling at me. "Huh?" I asked.

"Maybe you've noticed that I've been a little happier lately?"

I never really thought about whether my dad was happy. "I guess," I said. "I don't know."

"Well, Bobby," my father said, "Patrice and I have been dating for a little while now. I thought it was time that you met her."

I looked at Officer Kenyon—who looked almost as nervous as I was. Wait, I thought, she isn't here to arrest me? She's my father's girlfriend? I'm not going to jail! I was so relieved I felt like dancing on the table.

"That's the best news ever!" I shouted, a bit too excitedly. Then I tried to calm myself, "I mean, that's really great." I stood up from the table and backed away toward my room. "I'm pretty tired. Gonna get some sleep. Nice meeting you, Officer Kenyon," I said, knowing that my behavior probably seemed completely off the wall.

"Have a nice night," I said and then darted toward my room.

This had to be one of the strangest days of my life. I locked the door and crashed down onto my bed—exhausted. As soon as my head hit the pillow, questions started racing through my mind: Could I ever trust Jorge again, or look at him the same way? Would the next police car that I saw be the one looking for me? Who was my father's new girlfriend? Would Montezuma and the Tigres really call me back to the hideout to become one of them?

The final question was the one that kept me awake for the next hour or so:

Do I want to be a Tigre?

A week later, the word around the neighborhood was that Jorge had been arrested. I felt bad for my friend and was terrified I would be next. Around school, people were talking about what had happened at Mamacita's.

The good news was that every time someone told the story, their version of the events placed Jorge in the store without me. There must have been 10 versions of the story, and they all had one thing in common: My name was nowhere to be found in any of them.

I felt guilty about the whole thing. Even though I'd had no idea Jorge was going to steal money, we'd committed the crime together. I knew I was responsible, too. Yet he was going to jail, and I was in no trouble at all.

During all of elementary school and middle school and into my freshman year of high school, Raffy, Jorge and I had walked home together every day. We'd usually hang out at Raffy's and play video games. But just one week after the incident at Mamacita's, I was walking home from South Shore High School all alone.

Jorge had been arrested, and Raffy had been avoiding me. Raffy hated gangs and steered clear of the bad elements in our neighborhood. Now, I was the bad element he was staying away from.

I picked up a slice of pizza and ate it while I made my way home. Just as I finished the last cheesy bite, a cherry-red Buick lowrider pulled up beside me. The tinted window of the back passenger side rolled down. I recognized FDR from the Tigres' hideout immediately. He flashed a mischievous smile, completely different from the way he had greeted me when we first met. "Want a ride, homey?"

I looked around to make sure he was actually talking to me. "Nah, I'm good," I said, too scared to get into the car. I kept walking, but the car crawled along next to me.

"Come on, man. Come back to The Crib and hang out," FDR said. "We got some hot ladies up there." As he spoke, a beautiful Latina girl leaned over FDR and waved at me.

FDR continued, "You did real good, son. You kept your mouth shut. We respect that. Now come hang out with us."

I stopped and looked at the car. Part of me knew I should just run away. But there was another part that wanted to join the exciting world inside that car. I tried to speak in my toughest voice. "Montezuma said not to come back until he called me back," I said.

FDR smiled. A second later, the front passenger side window started to roll down. Montezuma practically filled up the whole window. "Get in the car," he said.

I decided I had no choice. I pulled open the back passenger door, climbing into the backseat. I was sitting next to FDR and his girlfriend. Guapo was driving, with Montezuma seated next to him.

Guapo looked at me through the rearview mirror and said, "So, your boy got bagged. He stood tall, though, and didn't rat on nobody."

I knew he was talking about Jorge, of course, and I just nodded.

"Want to know why you didn't get so much as a look from the cops? Even though Jorge's looking at a year or two in Horizon?" Guapo asked, referring to one of New York City's juvenile detention centers.

Of course I wanted to know. I nodded again.

Guapo pointed to Montezuma, who stared out the window. "That man right there. He makes sure that no Tigre ever acts like a rat, even when they go down."

I didn't know what to say. "Thank you," I mumbled.

"What's that?" Guapo asked.

"Thank you," I said a little louder.

I was shocked when the car screeched to a stop. Guapo turned back with fire in his eyes. "You think that's good enough? This man saw to it that your boy took the fall all by himself. You just say 'thank you'? Nah—you owe us, son."

I had no idea what would happen next. I was relieved when Montezuma put his hand up for Guapo to stop. "When I said I saw Tigre in you, Cortez, I meant it. Your friend got pinched, but there was no point in you going down, too," Montezuma said. "We're here now, to change your life. We're gonna bring you back to The Crib and initiate you as a Tigre tonight—if you're ready for it." I sat stunned for a moment. Finally, I spoke. "I don't know," I said. "I'm supposed to get home."

"If you don't want to roll with us now, you won't ever roll with us. It's your choice, homey," Guapo said.

My father's voice ran through my head. "Get out of the car, Roberto! This is your chance. You've worked too hard to throw it all away. Don't forget your plans and dreams. Be stronger than these fools, Roberto. Walk away."

I pictured him talking to me—the way he had ever since I was a kid—about how gangs were filled with cowards who ruined the neighborhood. I could hear him telling me that they ruined lives and made no apologies for it. But, in that moment, I just didn't see it that way. I loved my father. But I wanted to earn respect on my own, and have some fun, too. In the end, the idea of being a Tigre felt like something I just had to do.

"I'm in," I said, feeling the weight of the words as I spoke them.

Guapo smiled. "Good," he said. "Then let's go party."

We arrived at the Tigres' hideout just as the sun was beginning to set. This time, the Tigres greeted me differently. Everyone in the apartment came over, gave me a fist bump, and introduced themselves. I met "Tri-Go," "Steel Rod" and "Crunk." They congratulated me on not ratting on the gang or Jorge. It felt great to get respect from the Tigres.

Guapo stood in the middle of the living room and raised his voice so everyone could hear him. "Initiation time! Everyone get in here!" I had no idea what an initiation to the gang meant. The entire gang had come into the room. I was standing in the middle of a circle of about 15

Tigres. Most were drinking alcohol or smoking.

Crunk handed me a bottle of tequila. "You definitely want some of this before you get initiated, son. Take a couple of shots."

I'd never drunk alcohol before, even though some of my friends had. After all, I had been a track star and an A student. There's a first time for everything, I thought, taking a huge sip from the bottle. It tasted so strong that I could barely keep it down, but I swallowed hard. Then I drank some more. It didn't take long before I felt very lightheaded and a little sick.

I tried to pass the bottle back to Crunk, but he started screaming at me. "Drink!" he yelled. So I did, taking three or four more big sips. A short time later, I felt really sick and completely out of it.

"Don't puke, chico. We haven't even gotten started," Tri-Go said.

A moment later, the music started to play very loudly. The guys seemed to be getting more and more riled up. I saw FDR punch his fist into the palm of his hand excitedly. "It's on!" he screamed.

Then the lights went down. I watched Guapo move to the center of the room to address the group. Everyone huddled in a tighter circle with Guapo and me in the center. "All right, we got a new Tigre to bring in tonight." Guapo pulled an orange bandana from his back pocket and handed it to FDR. "Cover him up."

FDR came up behind me and blindfolded me. Guapo kept talking while I stood there, unable to see anything.

"When's your birthday?"

"January 22," I mumbled.

"Wrong!" Guapo said, and then addressed the group again. "Someone want to tell this boy his new birthday?"

"Today!" I heard a few voices call out.

"That's right," Guapo called out. "Your birthday is today—the day you are born into the Tigres. This is your new family, son. Your new name is 'Trece'—the most dangerous number. Bobby Cortez is dead. You have no other family, no other friends. You hear that, Trece?" ("Trece" means the number 13 in Spanish.)

"Yes," I nodded, and thought about my dad. I have a father who loves me. How could I trade him in for the Tigres? I wondered. Still, I knew it was too late to turn back.

I felt Guapo move in closer to me. He grabbed my neck and began screaming into my ear. He went through the gang's bylaws, which were the rules they lived by. He screamed about the police being the enemy. He talked about school being worthless. He yelled about how you always had to have another Tigre's back.

I was feeling sicker by the moment, and was doing everything I could to not throw up. Finally, Guapo loosened his grip on my neck, putting his arm around my shoulder and speaking into my ear. "You're one of us now, Trece. That means you do whatever you have to do for your Tigre brothers. You understand?"

"Yes," I said. I started to take the bandana off my face, thinking the initiation was over.

"Don't touch that bandana yet, Trece," Guapo said, adjusting my blindfold again. "The last part is the most important: blood in, blood out."

A moment later, I felt a huge blow to the side of my head. I hit the floor with a dull thud. I remember very little after that first punch. A lot of kicks, more punches, elbows and knees came from every member of the gang. By the end of it, I couldn't move.

The last thing I heard was Guapo's voice. "That's nothing compared to what we do to someone who betrays us. Welcome home, Trece."

I must've passed out after the beatdown, because when I woke up, it was nighttime. I tasted blood in my mouth and I still felt drunk. A few of the Tigres sat in the living room playing video games and drinking. It hurt to stand up.

"You survived your beatdown," FDR said. "Welcome to the Tigres, Trece."

Tri-Go extended his fist to me for a knuckle-bump. I could barely lift my arm to bump him back. He began laughing. "You had a nice little nap, Trece. I guess you liked that tequila, huh?"

CHAPTER SEVEN

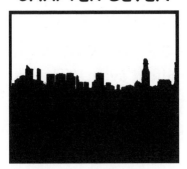

TWO BOBBYS

I was in a rush to leave The Crib. I knew I couldn't go into my house in my condition, so I headed over to Raffy's.

Raffy opened the door and scrunched up his face. "What happened to you?"

"Can I use your bathroom?" I asked, avoiding the question.

Raffy shrugged and opened the door for me to come in.

"I guess it's true, then, huh?" Raffy asked as he followed me toward the bathroom. "The rumors about you and Jorge being Tigres? Do you know they carry guns and sell drugs? You know how many of them end up dead or in jail. What are you thinking?"

"It's complicated, Raf," I said, shutting the door.

I stared in the mirror. I had two black eyes, dried blood was caked around my nose and mouth, and bruises covered my chest, arms and legs. I cleaned the blood off my face and walked out into Raffy's living room.

"You sure you're all right?" Raffy asked, more concerned than angry at this point.

I nodded. "Yeah, thanks."

Raffy followed me as I headed to the door. "I don't want to be around any Tigres, Bobby. So don't bring any of them around here, okay? And if you're one of them, then you shouldn't come around either."

A week ago, I never would've imagined I'd be having this conversation with my best friend. "Whatever," I said and stormed out the door.

When I returned home, my father and Patrice were cleaning the dishes. I stepped through the door quietly, trying to sneak past them. Unfortunately, we had a creaky door and Patrice looked up at me right as I entered the house. Of course, she noticed my face right away. "Oh—"

My father quickly came toward me, horrified. "What happened? Who did this?"

I didn't say a word.

"What happened?" he asked again. "Roberto?"

"I fell down some stairs," I said.

Patrice walked over to the freezer and started putting ice into an empty grocery bag. "Where did you fall?" he asked suspiciously.

"At Raffy's house. We were in the basement. The stairs are slippery," I answered.

"You got all those cuts and bruises from falling down the stairs?" Dad asked, obviously unconvinced. Patrice brought in a bag of ice and handed it to me. She and my father exchanged a concerned look. Then she left the room.

Dad put his hand on my shoulder. "Amigo, I'm gonna ask you again. What happened? Who beat you up?"

"Beat me up?" I said defensively. "Nobody. You think I can't take care of myself?" There was a part of me that wanted to tell my father the whole thing, but I didn't want to lose his respect.

"There's no shame in getting beat up. You're a good boy, Roberto, with a father who loves you. Not everyone is so lucky," he said. "Now, please, tell me what really happened."

"I already did. I fell down the stairs," I said. "Can I go to my room now?"

"Sure," he said, looking very concerned. He called out to me as I walked away, "We can talk about this tomorrow. Okay?"

I saw the disappointed look in my father's eyes. I hated lying to him, but I had no choice. It felt as if I were two different people. One part of me wanted to go to The Crib and tell them that I couldn't be in the gang. Losing my father's trust, and Raffy's friendship, wasn't worth it. Plus, I knew I could be sacrificing my future if I remained a member of the Tigres— and maybe even my life.

There was another part of me, though, that couldn't think of anything better than hanging out at The Crib. I thought of the girls that always seemed to be there. I thought of how cool it would look if I could drink next time without feeling sick. I thought about all the kids at school and how they would fear me. Being initiated into the Tigres made me feel like I was someone tough—someone special.

During the summer, that feeling of power didn't go away. I tried a lot of things I knew were wrong. But I was having too much fun to think any better of it. I could actually feel the difference when I walked around the neighborhood, too. I felt invincible.

It was hard to know how much my father knew about what I was doing. But, he definitely knew he couldn't stop me. Anytime he grounded me, I'd sneak out. I knew he loved me too much to kick me out of the house, even though part of me wished he would. That way, I could crash at The Crib every night, without having to lie to him as much.

There were two different Bobbys battling each other that summer. Most times, Trece-the-Tigre won out over pre-gang Bobby, the kid who listened to his father and stayed out of trouble.

But as the first day of school drew closer, I started to feel like I was in over my head. Most of the Tigres didn't go to school. And if they did, they went just to cause trouble. I still wanted to do something with my life. I wanted to go to college, maybe even run on the track team. But I never dared tell a fellow Tigre that. I wasn't sure exactly how or when my time in the gang would end. But I definitely knew that something had to give.

One afternoon late that summer, FDR informed me that we were going to "throw down" with the Aviadors. They were another local gang. They had been disrespecting members of the Tigres. Montezuma decided we would settle it once and for all—and earn back our respect.

"Tomorrow night," FDR said. "We're meeting at The Crib at 9:30. Don't worry, though. We're gonna shoot the fair one. No weapons."

I breathed a big sigh of relief, even though the idea of a fair fight scared the heck out of me, too.

I spent the next day at Shea Stadium, where the Mets played, with my dad. Getting out of Skypoint and away from the Tigres was just what the doctor ordered. My dad was still one of my favorite people in the world, although I could never admit that to my gang friends. Dad and I had a great time for most of the day.

He talked about Patrice a lot that day. This made me curious about whether they might get married, so I asked him.

"We're not planning to right now. But she is the type of person, like your mother, that I could see wanting to be in our lives every day."

A lot of kids are freaked out by their parents dating, but I wanted to be cool. It was good to see my dad happy. If Patrice was the reason for that happiness, that was fine by me.

Later on, just after the Mets took a 6-5 lead in the sixth inning, my dad turned serious. "Roberto, I need to talk to you. Ever since that night you came home with all of those bruises, I feel like you've been keeping things from me. I know you've been lying to me, too. I miss the old Bobby. I don't understand what's happened to you."

"Nothing has happened," I muttered. Then, my eyes locked with my father's. We shared an intense moment, and I decided that I would tell him everything. I would tell him that I had joined a gang. I would beg for his forgiveness. I would ask for his help. I would tell him how I had started thinking about quitting the Tigres, but how I was afraid of the danger I'd be in if I actually did. I would ask him for his advice on how to get control of my life again.

Just as these words were about to pour out of my mouth, I chickened out. I broke free from his stare and said, "Like I told you, I fell down the stairs. I'm all grown up—I think you just need to accept the fact that I'm not a little boy anymore."

We barely spoke during the next three innings. After the game, and the quiet train ride home, I headed to The Crib.

CHAPTER EIGHT

TIGRES VS. AVIADORS

By the time I got to The Crib, all the Tigres were ready to leave for the fight at the P.S. 212 schoolyard. Most of them had been chilling at The Crib for the past few hours, drinking and getting pumped up for the fight. Sixteen of us left that night—ready to take on the Aviadors.

Montezuma led the way. The calm look he normally carried on his face was replaced by a fierce and violent expression.

Some of the other Tigres weaved through the group as we walked, unable to contain their excitement. FDR grabbed my shoulders and said, "You ready to fight, Trece?"

I wasn't ready at all. I didn't even know what the other gang had done to us. Or what we had done to them. All I knew was that Guapo had some beef with Oso, the leader of the Aviadors. FDR asked me again, "You ready, son?"

"Hell yeah," I said, faking confidence.

"Good," FDR said, "'cause last time we rumbled, one of our boys wound up dead. Tonight, we get revenge!" My heart sank in my chest. I hadn't thought very much about getting killed. Sure, I realized that people would most likely get hurt tonight, maybe even me. But someone ending up dead wasn't something I knew how to deal with.

It may have been fear that made things clear for me in that moment. But I finally grasped how bad my decisions from over the summer really were. The impact they could have on the rest of my life suddenly felt way too real. I looked around at my fellow Tigres and started to see many of them for who they were—a group of misguided teens. They'd turned into violent criminals with little care for anyone but themselves. What am I doing with these guys? I wondered.

We approached the schoolyard and Montezuma looked angrier than ever. Guapo, meanwhile, was looking more and more like a madman. He was screaming about how much damage we were about to do. I stood directly behind him and noticed that a gun was tucked into the back of his pants. FDR had said we'd be "shooting the fair one." So why was Guapo packin' heat? I wondered.

We turned the corner into the P.S. 212 schoolyard, a place known for gang activity, especially at night. This was the place Skypoint's 'hoods came to fight. A large group of

Aviadors were waiting for us, wearing their gold and green colors. Guapo turned back and looked at the group of Tigres. "You guys ready? 'Zuma, you ready?" Montezuma nodded and led the Tigres forward. He was like a football coach leading his team onto the field, except we weren't playing a game. This was real life.

All I knew was that I wanted no part in this fight. I had no idea how to get out of it, though. If I ran away, there'd be hell to pay the next time I saw the Tigres. They'd probably kill me.

My life from three months earlier started to flash before my eyes. I thought of Raffy, the track team, my college dreams—it all seemed so perfect, yet so far away.

"What's up?" Oso yelled toward Montezuma, snapping me quickly from my daydream.

Montezuma didn't respond and moved in closer to the group of Aviadors. My concerns suddenly turned into all-out panic. I had to think fast. I looked over toward the dumpsters that sat right against the outside wall of the school. They were about 20 yards away from where the Aviadors stood and slightly hidden from view. Could I hide there without being seen?

Things were heating up. I moved in closer with the rest of the Tigres, still looking for a way to escape. Both sides started yelling at one another as the distance between the groups shrunk.

Finally, Guapo walked right up to Oso. The Aviadors' leader wore a mean scowl. The two men stared into each other's eyes. The tension in the air was thick. I took a small step backward.

Then, like a flash of lightning, Montezuma stepped to the front of the pack, pushing Guapo aside. He grabbed Oso and leveled him with a crushing punch. Just like that, it was on.

Within a few seconds, nearly every member of the two gangs was engaged with another. Two Aviators were kicking Steel Rod when they turned their eyes onto me. One of them grabbed my left shoulder and took a swing at me. I ducked and he missed. Acting on instinct, I wound up with my right hand and threw the first real punch I'd ever thrown. It landed, hitting the Aviador squarely in the cheek.

The guy I'd hit started toward me again—much angrier now. Just before he reached back to hit me, I noticed that he looked familiar. He stopped in his tracks. "Bobby?" It was Tomas Rodriguez. His father and my father were close friends. I remembered my father telling me how Mr. Rodriguez was worried about his son—thinking he might have gotten mixed up in a gang. I remembered how sad that made my father. Tomas had been at my house a bunch of times when I was younger, and he was always nice to me. He was one of the last people in the world I'd ever want to punch.

"Tomas, I didn't know that was you. I gotta go,

man."

"Go then," he said, pretending to push me backward. "I won't say anything."

In the chaos of the fight, I bolted for the dumpster. I knew I couldn't get out of the schoolyard without anyone seeing. My dash to safety left Tomas holding his own as he fought off FDR. Although we were members of two different gangs, I didn't want to see anything happen to my old friend. I had never felt so upset in my life.

I tried to catch my breath, hoping nobody could see me. After a few moments, I exhaled and nearly threw up. There was a pay phone on the wall about 10 yards away from me. I desperately wanted to call my father.

A minute or two later, I peeked out to look at the fight. At this point, most of the Tigres were lying on the ground. They'd been beaten up pretty badly. Montezuma was the last Tigre standing, fending off three of the Aviadors. Eventually, four and then five of them jumped Montezuma, finally bringing him to the ground.

Around 10 Aviadors milled around the Tigres. They were waving their gang signs, giving each other pounds and talking a lot of trash. Some of them—like Tomas—had already left. Clearly, they had won the fight. I watched as the rest of them started to head triumphantly toward the schoolyard exit.

Then I saw Guapo, bloodied and beaten, stand up and yell at them. "You ain't so hard. You guys just had more heads than us today."

The rival group stopped walking. They turned toward Guapo. "Shut your mouth, punk!" one of them yelled out.

I was shocked to see Guapo respond by marching toward the group of Aviadors, alone. When he got about 5 feet from them, he pulled the gun from his pants. I could barely watch, afraid someone was about to get shot.

"Who's a punk now?" he asked, pointing the gun at the group.

Montezuma yelled out after him, "Guapo, put it away!" Then he got to his feet and started walking toward Guapo. The rest of the Tigres started running toward the exit. I watched from my hiding spot, frozen with fear.

Some of the Aviadors also started to scatter in different directions. Three of them, though, including Oso, pulled out guns and trained them on Guapo. "We said we were shooting the fair one," Oso said to Guapo. "But you pulled a gun on us after you got beat fair and square. That ain't right, yo. Throw your gun on the ground and get out of here before I put a hole in your face."

Knowing he was outmanned, Guapo bent down and left his gun on the ground.

Oso pointed his gun at Montezuma next. "You stay right where you are."

Without looking Montezuma in the face, Guapo ran from the schoolyard. He left the leader of the Tigres with the angry Aviators.

With his gun touching Montezuma's forehead, Oso began to yell. "This was supposed to be a fair fight," he screamed. "But your boy didn't play by the rules. So now you've got to pay for it!"

Montezuma hadn't even been the one to bring the gun. But I knew there was a chance he wouldn't make it out of the schoolyard alive. I had to do something. I dug my nails into the palm of my hand as I looked over at the pay phone again. If Oso saw me, I was dead for sure. Plus, if I called for help and anyone found out it was me, they would likely kill me for that, too.

On the other hand, I couldn't just stand by and watch another human being get murdered, could I?

Oso continued yelling. "You've been bossing everyone in this neighborhood around for too long, 'Zuma." He swung his pistol against Montezuma's cheek, knocking him to the ground.

My eyes focused on the pay phone. I bolted over to the phone as fast as I could—risking my life in the process. I knew that if there was any of the old Bobby Cortez left inside of me, then I had to act.

When I reached the phone, I looked over my shoulder again. Nobody had noticed me. At this point, I probably could have escaped the schoolyard to the safety of the open street. But I chose to do what I knew was right. I chose to save Montezuma's life and end my time in the gang—permanently.

I picked up the phone and knew that Trece was no longer a part of my life. After tonight, Bobby Cortez would officially be enemy number one of the Aviadors and the Tigres.

The rival gangbangers took turns kicking Montezuma. If I wasted another minute, he would likely end up dead. I slid a quarter into the phone. "Hello," the voice at the other end answered.

My voice cracked, "Dad?"

"Roberto? Is everything all right?" he asked.

"No, Dad. I'm at the 212 schoolyard, and they're beating up someone real bad. They're going to kill him," I said.

He asked in a panicked voice, "Who's beating up who?"

"A gang, Dad. They're beating up the leader of the Tigres, and I need your help." Then I blurted out the words I had wanted to confess to my father for months. "I'm in the gang, too, Dad."

I couldn't imagine what he must have thought of me. He must have been piecing together the bruises, my strange behavior and this call—and probably losing any respect for me that he had left. The real respect, too, the kind you earned over time by proving yourself.

"I'll be right there, Roberto," he said.

I hung up the phone and felt like a huge weight had

been lifted off me. That feeling didn't last long, though. As I was running back to my spot by the dumpsters, I watched Oso land a vicious kick to Montezuma's head. It leveled him and he stopped moving.

I heard another angry scream and looked up to see that Oso hadn't stopped kicking. I decided that I'd seen enough. Guapo's gun was on the ground a few feet away from me. Although I had never held a gun, I ran full speed toward the weapon and grabbed it.

"The cops are coming!" I shouted. Then, to show the Aviadors that I wasn't trying to shoot at them, I pointed the gun high in the air. I fired it five times toward the sky. In a matter of moments, all the Aviadors sprinted out of the schoolyard. They left Montezuma in a bloody heap.

About one minute later four police cars and an ambulance arrived. I watched the EMTs run toward Montezuma and begin tending to him. It was over.

I felt so lucky—lucky to be alive, and lucky to have a father I could call in this situation. I knew that most of the kids in the Tigres and the Aviadors didn't have enough people steering them away from scenes like this one. I promised myself that I would do whatever I could to stop someone else from making the same mistakes that I'd made. If I had to, I would devote my life to this task.

My father's Chevrolet pulled up behind the cop cars. He strode toward me, walking quickly across the schoolyard. Patrice followed behind him. I ran toward him as fast as I could. We met in the middle of the yard and he wrapped me in a tight hug.

Two medics and a group of cops passed right behind us, rolling Montezuma toward an ambulance. He was a wanted man in Brooklyn, but had been hiding in the shadows from police for years. Thanks to me, they finally got him.

"Watch your back, Trece," Montezuma hissed as he passed by.

The ride home with my father and Patrice was difficult. I felt so much guilt about the way I had treated both of them, particularly my dad.

"Did you know Mason Torres, the guy who got beat up, Bobby?" Patrice asked, interrupting my thoughts.

I was done lying. "Yes. We call him Montezuma, though."

"How the hell did you get mixed up with a gang?" my father said. "You're a good boy, Roberto."

"I don't know, it just kind of happened, Dad," I said, not knowing how to explain.

Patrice stepped in and helped me. "These local gangs reel in kids like Bobby slowly. They show them the violence and drugs little by little, until they're so deep into it that it all seems normal," Patrice said. Then she looked back at me sternly. "I'm not making excuses for you, Bobby. You made terrible choices. I just hope you see the light now."

"I do," I replied. "I really do."

My father shook his head and looked at me through the rearview mirror. "Well, this is the end of it. You're not going anywhere except school for the next year."

"It's not that simple," Patrice said. "After tonight, Bobby's not going to be safe in Brooklyn anymore. They'll come after him."

"So what do we do now?" he asked, but Patrice didn't answer. No one spoke for the rest of the ride home.

When we pulled into the driveway of our house, my dad didn't get out of the car. Instead he asked Patrice to give the two of us a moment alone. We sat silently for about five minutes before my father spoke. "I'm glad you called me, Roberto. That was very brave."

"No, it wasn't," I said, nearly crying. "I screwed up my life pretty bad, huh?"

"At least you're alive. I'll figure out a way to keep you safe. We'll start a new life if we have to."

"I'm so sorry I let you down," I said.

"You just got lost—but you found your way back. And that's what counts."

When I went to sleep that night—with two armed police officers guarding the front door of my house—I swore that I'd never get lost again. Nothing was going to stand in the way of my becoming the man I wanted to be, a man like my father.

CHAPTER NINE

A NEW LIFE

Life changed a lot after that night. Staying in Brooklyn was no longer an option. The Tigres were hunting me, and if they found me, I was as good as dead. My father had a cousin, Carlos Nolasco, who lived upstate. Dad called him that night, asking about jobs. As luck would have it, Carlos needed a foreman for his construction company. Dad happily accepted a job offer.

Nolasco Construction was located in Buffalo, New York, which is about eight hours northwest of New York City. Moving there would put some safe distance between me and the Tigres. I took the long bus ride upstate the very next morning to start my new life. Patrice drove me to the bus station at 4 in the morning, so nobody would see where I was headed. I stayed with cousin Carlos for a few weeks while Dad got everything arranged for our secret move.

Over the next few years, I went to high school in

Buffalo and graduated near the top of my class. I never heard from the Tigres, or anyone else from Skypoint, again. I lost touch with Raffy. I hoped Jorge had managed to turn his life around, but figured I would never know for sure.

I was glad to have grown up in Brooklyn, but I also came to love Buffalo. Not many kids from where I grew up had the chance to ski, snowboard, kayak, attend Buffalo Bills games, and visit cool international cities like Toronto and Montreal. There was something magically different about my life upstate.

The worst part of moving was that my dad and Patrice broke up shortly afterward. Although Dad never let me take the blame, I knew it was my fault. The distance was simply too much for them to overcome.

Despite his love life failing, Dad was doing really well at work. He was making more money and really enjoyed what he was doing. Carlos and his wife had us over for dinner often, and it felt great to be with family.

As for me, I was thriving. My favorite class in high school became criminology, where we read all sorts of police stories. Law enforcement had always interested me— especially since escaping gang life.

I got a cool job during my senior year in high school, tutoring kids from some of Buffalo's rougher neighborhoods. This was my first step toward making a positive impact in the lives of potential gang members.

After high school, I attended the Shreeveboro College of Criminal Justice in western Pennsylvania. Staying in the dorms was quite an experience. You can't beat all-night Xbox marathons—or having smart and beautiful girls living right next door to you.

I made more friends during my freshman year of college than I'd made during my entire life up until then. I even met a few people who'd been tempted by gangs and turned their lives around, the same way I had. Those of us who had lived through gang life had sad stories to tell—and friends we'd lost along the way.

Many of my classmates went on to work in police departments around the country. I wanted to fight crime at the highest level. That meant joining the Federal Bureau of Investigation—the FBI. The FBI is arguably the most elite crime-fighting force in the world. The Bureau wanted candidates with diverse work experience, so I spent four years teaching at my old high school in Buffalo.

Keeping good kids away from gangs wasn't always a battle I could win. I watched some of my best students fall into gang life during high school. A few times I was able to help draw them out, but other times, I lost them.

Finally, I was ready to apply for the FBI. Despite my excellent grades, I doubted if I would make it through their tough admissions process. After all, my history wasn't exactly squeaky clean. But despite my past, I was invited to attend training at the FBI Academy in Quantico, Virginia.

The night before I headed to Quantico was my 27th birthday. Dad and I went to dinner in Buffalo. Dad never looked so proud. "Your mother is smiling in heaven, Roberto," he told me.

There's no way to understand the commitment an agent is asked to make until the moment you're sitting at the training orientation. I would have access to more technology than I ever could've imagined—not just to keep our country safe from gangs, but from all sorts of organized crime and terrorism.

On day one, my classmates and I sat in the 1,000-seat auditorium. We listened to a presentation on the core principles of the Bureau: obedience to the Constitution of the United States, respect for the dignity of all those we protect, compassion, fairness, and uncompromising personal and institutional integrity. Hearing them, and looking at the other focused individuals around me, confirmed that this elite group was something I was born to be a part of.

The next 17 weeks were an exhausting combination of training and testing. The biggest complaint among us "NATS" (short for New Agent Trainees) was about how much time we had to spend in the classroom. It felt like high school all over again. We took written tests on things like behavioral science, law, and interviewing and interrogation techniques. We learned about ethics, investigation and forensic science (which is the science used on physical evidence relating to a criminal case).

There were also plenty of "PT" tests, which is short for physical training. They made us do more sit-ups, push-ups and running than I'd ever done in my life. Then, we were tested on "DT," which is short for defensive tactics. We learned techniques for disarming criminals who might be holding a gun or a knife. We learned how to deal with other physical situations we might face in the field.

The most memorable part was the work we did at Hogan's Alley, a fake city built just for FBI training. They'd throw us into the pretend world of Hogan's Alley to practice what we'd learned. It was like a giant movie set, with a fake post office and drugstore. There were even actors who were hired to create a city environment. During one exercise, we were called in to investigate a "bank robbery."

As we were collecting evidence at the Bank of Hogan, the robbers surprised us by coming back and shooting in our direction. Even though the bullets were really just pellets of colored paint, we had to act like the threat was real. Our grade, and perhaps our graduation, would depend on how well we handled the situation.

When the flurry of "bullets" began, I took cover under a desk near the bank's door. Then I chased one of the robbers into the street. Running as fast as I ever had, I caught up to him. Instead of trying to grab him, I used a technique I'd learned in class called the "steam pipe." I pushed him forward with enough force to make him fall to the ground, using his own momentum against him. Then, I used a "double leverage reversal" to pin the hand he held his gun with against the ground. I easily got his weapon away and then handcuffed him.

No one scores perfectly on every aspect of their exams at the Academy. But I was one of the top applicants of the year.

On graduation day, I thought about how differently it felt to pledge my loyalty to the FBI than when I joined the Tigres.

CHAPTER TEN

BACK IN SKYPOINT

My journey had come full circle. Thirteen years after running from the Tigres, I was back in Brooklyn. During my first week on the job as an FBI agent, an anonymous tip had led me to my old neighborhood—Skypoint. I had returned to the theater I had sat inside for at least a hundred movies during my youth. I then made my way onto the rooftops, where I chased a gang member in a white hoodie.

The next morning, while sitting in Director Mc-Dowell's office, I felt like my life was starting to make sense. I was an FBI agent, chasing down the same misfits that had nearly ruined my life 14 years earlier. I was doing exactly what I was always meant to do.

But when I was handed a particular photograph, my emotions were turned upside down. I held it in my hand. I didn't want to believe that the familiar face staring back at me was the same man who may have committed the murder at the Skypoint Theater.

"Hey, Rookie," Tim said. "Are you still with us?"

Tim and Director McDowell were waiting for me to say something, but I was in shock. "Sorry," I said. "I'm just—"

"I understand you knew the man in that photo a long time ago, Cortez," McDowell said.

I nodded. "He was my best friend."

Tim shot me a strange look. He was confused about how or why I knew the head of the Tigres.

McDowell continued, "Along with whoever killed the guy in that old movie theater, this is the man I want you to bring in. But it's not going to be easy. The Tigres have grown up—they've been classified as 'organized crime' now. That's why the Bureau is handling this, and not the NYPD. This man is a big reason parents don't feel safe letting their kids play on the streets of Skypoint anymore. The same streets you grew up on, Cortez."

"I thought you grew up in Buffalo," Tim said, still confused.

"I did. I mean, I lived in Buffalo for a long time," I said. "But I was raised in Skypoint."

I flipped through the rest of the photos in the stack McDowell had given me. Most were of the murder scene at the Skypoint Theater.

In the first photo, a man in his 20s lay dead. His baggy jeans had the pockets pulled inside out. He was wearing an authentic throwback Patrick Ewing jersey and had gold chains around his neck. He wore a brand-new pair of Nikes with fresh-looking dirt on the bottoms. He'd been shot twice and his throat was slashed. This was the man I nearly tripped over in the projector room.

The next photo showed the back wall of the same room. The Tigres' motto was spray painted in bright orange: "Mordida Feroz," which means vicious bite.

"That's their gang tag up there on the wall," I said.

"Yup," McDowell confirmed. "Same tag on the can of spray paint."

"Maybe this guy just ran into some Tigres looking to rob someone," I said, trying to piece everything together.

Tim shook his head.

"You don't think so?" McDowell asked, raising an eyebrow at Tim.

Tim pointed to the photo. "That jersey is worth at least 200 bucks, and those jeans are probably 150. The shoes are maybe another 150. Plus, look at all the gold around his neck. Those chains are probably worth a couple of G's," he said.

"Are you trying out for 'The Price Is Right' or are we solving a murder case, Tim?" I asked.

Tim didn't see the humor in my joke. "Let me ask you a question, Cortez. Why would anybody rob someone, take the time to drag them into an abandoned movie theater before killing them, and then leave a bunch of valu-ables on them?" he asked. "That doesn't make sense."

I knew that Tim was probably right.

"Let's go back and take another look at the crime scene. There's more to this than a robbery," Tim said.

"Great idea," I said sarcastically. After all, I was the one who wanted to go back to the crime scene yesterday.

McDowell had something to say before we left his office: "You may not want to hear this, Cortez. But right now you know more about the Tigres than you do about the FBI. If you and Tim work together, I think you can crack this case. So, instead of trying to leap over buildings, use your knowledge of gang life. Try to learn something about the way police work really gets done. And O'Rourke, take it easy on the kid and listen to what he has to say—he knows this world better than you do."

"Yes, sir," Tim said.

We left McDowell's office and headed toward Tim's car. We passed a gorgeous blond-haired woman. I almost stopped dead in my tracks. She might have been the most beautiful woman I'd ever seen. "Who is that?" I asked Tim.

"Out of your league," he said.

"Out of your league, maybe," I muttered. "Keep in mind, we're in different leagues, O'Rourke. I'm in the un-der-50 league."

Tim laughed at my joke. It was the first time I had

made my partner laugh, and it made me feel good. "Her name is Saunders, Rook," Tim said, loosening up a bit. "She's a tech agent on the 11th floor. And I'm only 48."

I got into the car and sank into my seat. I felt about as useful to the FBI as a pile of rocks. I had totally misread my first crime scene—luckily, Tim hadn't.

As we drove back to the theater, I had to remind myself that in front of me was a great opportunity: Chasing the Tigres was my chance to make something good out of the biggest mistake of my life. Even if it meant putting my old friend behind bars. I think Tim could tell I was wrestling with some strange feelings. He tried to strike up a conversation.

"You really used to be a Tigre?" he asked.

"Yup," I nodded. "A long time ago, though. I was 14."

"And the guy in the picture, the head of the gang? Did he recruit you?" he asked.

"No," I said. "No way. He wasn't involved in the gang at all back then. He's actually the last guy I would ever think of as being in a gang."

"Really?" Tim asked.

"Yup," I nodded. "Obviously, he's a different person now than the kid I knew back in the day."

I looked down at the picture again. If it had been Jorge staring back at me, I wouldn't have been nearly as surprised. After all, he was involved with the Tigres years ago. But it was shocking to learn that paranoid bookworm Raffy had become the head of the Tigres.

Tim's car came to a stop in front of the Skypoint Theater. We headed in. Two NYPD officers stepped aside as we flashed our badges and ducked under the yellow police tape.

We walked into the projector room, where I'd found the dead man. This time, there were lights illuminating the scene. Everything was the same—except for the body, of course. It had been taken to the coroner's office.

There were a few other investigators working at the scene, taking photos and dusting for prints. Tim introduced me to Paul Wilson, an NYPD C.S.I. guy. "Detective Wilson, this is the rookie, Agent Cortez—we call him Spiderman."

Detective Wilson shook my hand and laughed. "I guess you're the kid who jumped across the rooftops yesterday. We heard all about that. Nice to meet you, Spidey."

I shook his hand and faked a smile. "You too." I was too focused on looking at my first real murder scene to be annoyed. This was typical rookie hazing. I knew I would have to put up with some of it.

At a crime scene, it's critical that no clue be missed. But the hardest part is to know what you are looking for. There was a chalk outline of the body. Flags had been placed next to each piece of evidence.

I noticed a crumpled paper bag with blood on it,

right in the middle of the chalk outline. I walked over and took a closer look. I motioned for Tim to come over. "The bag has blood on it," I said. "Looks like the body fell onto it."

"Yup," Tim said, not interested. "They flagged it—nothing much there."

Detective Wilson stood next to Tim. He seemed vaguely interested in our conversation.

A few inches away, I saw several rubber bands strewn across the floor. "Have these been tested?" I asked.

"Tested for what?" Wilson asked.

Tim stepped closer to me and spoke so only I could hear him, "Listen, Rook, you can't just walk in here and start telling experienced cops who have been looking at crime scenes since you were watching cartoons about—"

I cut him off, refusing to be intimidated. "If you test these rubber bands, you'll find residue of cash and possibly drugs," I said. "The Tigres transport cash in tight rolls wrapped in rubber bands. They carry the rolls in brown paper bags like that one—and they usually carry drugs in the same bag."

"Are you sure?" Tim asked, clearly excited about this potential clue.

"That's the way they did it back in the day," I said, taking a few steps back to look at the whole scene.

"I'll check it out," Wilson said. "Nice work, Spider-man."

I was trying hard to put all of the information together. We had a body, found in an abandoned movie theater. There was a gang motto spray painted on the wall. It didn't appear to be a robbery because none of the victim's expensive clothing or jewelry had been stolen. I also saw the clumps of dirt that had fallen from his otherwise-clean sneakers. What did it all mean?

Just then, something clicked. "What if it's a message?" I asked, piecing together my theory as I spoke. "What if this guy stole money from the Tigres? Money that was being held in the paper bag. Maybe they chased him, probably through Bayline Park. That's why he had mud on his shoes. They probably chased him all the way here to Avenue L. They caught up with him, dragged him into the theater, and took back the cash he'd stolen."

"I'm listening," Tim said.

I continued, getting more excited as I spoke. "Then they killed him and left him here, knowing that the body would be found. They were sending a message, Tim. That guy in the hoodie that I chased—he came back to the murder scene just to spray paint the gang tag on the wall. That was a huge risk. He did it because somebody high up in the Tigres wanted the entire neighborhood to know who killed this man. He wanted to let them know what happens when you steal from the Tigres."

"But spray painting the gang tag tells the cops who's responsible, too," Tim said. "That sounds pretty stupid."

"Not really. Even if they didn't spray paint their tag, every cop still would have thought of the Tigres as the number one suspect for this murder. They're not trying to hide the fact that they're killers anymore. Plus, they know that everyone in the neighborhood is too scared to do anything to help bring them down. The Tigres aren't scared of the law because they've had no reason to be."

"Except now they do, because we've got a secret weapon," Tim said.

"What's that?" I asked.

"We've got you now," he said, patting me on the back. "The ex-Tigre."

I smiled. Maybe Tim wasn't all that bad. "So, now what?" I asked.

"We need some more evidence. We've gotta find a kid just like you were," Tim said.

"Huh?" I asked, chasing Tim out of the projector room and down the stairs.

"Gangs like the Tigres thrive by recruiting kids like you," he said. "Over time, the violence, the drugs, all that crap, becomes normal. Then these kids become the gang leaders of tomorrow."

Tim had a point. Back when I knew Raffy, he hadn't so much as seen a drug, and he wouldn't have killed a spider. Now, he was the head of a gang that sold drugs and killed people.

"We need to grab a kid new to the Tigres. If we

push him, I bet he'll lead us to the people close to the top, if not right to Raffy himself."

"You're crazy if you think one of these kids is gonna talk to us," I said.

"We're just gonna have to go fishing tomorrow."

"Fishing?" I asked, confused.

Tim smiled. "Yeah, sometimes you gotta stand right outside the water waiting for something to bite," he said.

CHAPTER ELEVEN

A FISHING TRIP

Later that morning, we sat in Tim's car outside of Bayline Park. We were waiting to see something we could move on. We were parked with a good view of a heavily wooded area where gang members hung out.

The youngest members of the Tigres were usually tasked with hanging out in the park. They sold drugs to whoever came around looking for them. They'd stand around with their orange bandanas in their back pockets. They were walking advertisements for the fact that they were selling drugs. Still, they had a system that kept the local police away.

The kids wouldn't carry drugs on them normally. That way, if they were stopped by the police, they couldn't be arrested. They'd take money from customers in return for someone's beeper number. The customer would later beep a delivery person who would arrange a meet-up. Since no one in the neighborhood would dare rat out the gang, the local cops couldn't do much about it. I told Tim that finding a Tigre with drugs on him was rare.

"So is catching a 30-pound trout," Tim said, "but it's not impossible."

We sat in the car for several hours—fishing for a sketchy-looking Tigre who might be carrying drugs. In between stories about his father and grandfathers, Tim explained how careful we needed to be. While we wanted information from one of the young Tigres, we didn't want blood on our hands. I knew firsthand that a gang member who talked to police could easily wind up dead.

Soon, we noticed a teenager leave the park. He was nervously looking around in every direction. Then he flipped up his hood. He even tucked his orange bandana all the way into his back pocket so it was out of sight.

"You see what I see?" Tim said.

"A 30-pound trout?" I asked.

"I don't know," Tim said. "But he looks like he's got something he isn't supposed to."

I unlocked the car door ready to pounce. Tim locked it again and started the car. "Let's follow him a few blocks," he said. "We have to do this right. If another Tigre sees him get in this car, it's over for that kid. And that'll be on us."

I appreciated Tim's cautious approach. Tim pulled the car out and followed the kid as he walked up Bayline Avenue. The kid was probably about 15. He walked toward the Pinewood Projects, but stopped into the market at the nearby gas station. Tim pulled the car up to one of the pumps and got out. "Stay here," he said, heading into the store.

I watched through the window as Tim stood behind the young Tigre in line. The kid paid the cashier for a Coke and some candy. Then he walked outside with Tim right behind him. When the kid passed by our car, Tim grabbed him by the shoulder. He leaned his head down and whispered something into the kid's ear.

The kid shook his head "no," and Tim gestured toward the car. The kid looked for a second like he was going to get in. Then he spun away and started a full-on sprint in the opposite direction. Tim started after him, but within a few steps, the kid had opened up a lead.

Tim might know a lot about being an FBI special agent. But he probably wouldn't be able to pass the PT exams at the Academy any longer. I hustled out of the car and watched the kid jump a fence and cut up the street. Then I raced past Tim and told him to meet me around the corner with the car.

I hopped the fence and continued down 96th Street. I turned up my speed and moved as fast as I could behind the kid. I gained on him as he headed toward the next street, which was the back side of a row of stores.

It didn't take long for me to close the gap between us to about 30 feet. Nearing the end of the street, the kid turned to look back. I could tell by his face that he was surprised I'd gotten so close. Just as he'd turned to look at me, a huge garbage truck roared around the corner. The truck was about to crush the kid.

I pointed at the truck, but the kid just looked at me. The driver saw me but didn't seem to notice the kid. I waved my arms for him to stop.

When the young Tigre turned and finally saw the truck, he was only a few feet away from being hit. He totally froze.

Now the driver saw him and jammed on his brakes—but garbage trucks don't stop on a dime. I reached out and grabbed the kid by his book bag, throwing him out of the way. Then I slid underneath the truck like a baseball player trying to beat a perfect throw home. I flattened my body as much as I could against the pavement. The truck skidded over my body, without touching me. The truck stopped with the bumper right over my waist.

I quickly got up and ran over to the young Tigre, who was too shocked to move. I was able to get him into cuffs. "You almost got us both killed. But nobody outruns Bobby Cortez, kid," I said with a smile.

Checking his back pockets, I pulled out a bag carrying about an ounce of marijuana. "Gotcha," I said. This was more than enough to turn him over to the local cops. I called Tim on my cell phone, and a minute later he pulled up. We loaded the kid into the back of the car.

As I caught my breath, Tim parked the car on a secluded street behind the park. He looked through the rearview at the kid. We'd gotten lucky to find a Tigre with drugs on him. Tim's hunch had been dead on.

"You ready to answer some questions for me?" Tim asked.

"I don't talk to cops," he said.

"Well, we're not cops. We're from the FBI. Do you talk to federal agents?" I asked.

Tim took the bag from my hand. "You see this?" he said. "If you talk to us, this goes down the sewer and a lot of problems go away for you."

"Why should I believe you?" he asked.

"Believe this, kid," Tim said. "If you don't talk, I'll arrest you right now for possession with intent to distribute. So, it's up to you."

It took a while for the kid to start talking. But after a few minutes, we had him answering all of our questions. His name was Miguel, and he had only been in the Tigres for five months. He didn't want to go to jail, but he didn't want to end up dead either. Every time he answered a question, he followed by saying, "They're gonna kill me for telling you that."

We calmed the kid down and let him know we'd keep him safe. Then we showed him the murder scene in the photograph. He identified the corpse as a local high school dropout named Julio Valdez. Julio had robbed a few younger Tigres for their drug money, he told us.

Miguel hadn't known about the murder. This was obvious from the way his eyes bugged out of his head when he saw the picture. Most younger gang members weren't told all of the nasty business of the Tigres.

We asked where we could find Raffy, who Miguel called "Espectro." He said he didn't know. Raffy's gang name, Espectro, translated to "ghost," which was proving to be an accurate description for him. Raffy had no known addresses and was living off the grid while running the Tigres. I knew how intelligent Raffy was, so I understood that catching him wouldn't be easy.

"Where do you get your drugs from?" Tim asked Miguel.

"C'mon, he'll kill me," he said. Then, he answered quietly, "Guapo."

My eyes widened. "Guapo?" I asked.

"He's captain, right under Espectro," Miguel said.

I couldn't believe that, after all these years, Guapo was still second in command of the Tigres.

"Does he still live in the Pinewood Projects?" I asked.

The kid nodded. Before we let him go, I gave him a short talk about how I'd gotten out of the Tigres and that he could, too.

The next day, we parked outside the Pinewood Projects. They were a set of apartment buildings housing thousands of Skypoint's residents. Years ago, this was a safe place to live. But as Skypoint began to give way to the Tigres, housing projects like Pinewood became ground zero for gang activity. The residents lived in fear, not just of gangs, but of the police as well. Talking to police could mean ending up dead, at the hands of a gang member.

Tim and I knew we needed to corner Guapo inside a contained space so he couldn't escape. Just outside Guapo's building were two kids playing stickball. Even though we were dressed in street clothes, I heard one say "policia" to the other, pointing at us.

We entered building 11, walked up to the third floor and found a perfect spot at a hallway window. It overlooked the entrance to the building. We got comfortable and waited. We endured dirty looks from residents who were nervous about two men sitting in their hallway, most likely with badges and guns in their pockets.

While we waited, Tim and I continued getting to know each other better. Even though Tim had grown up in Connecticut, while I'd been raised in Skypoint, our views on the world weren't all that different. We both idolized our dads, and Tim was a Mets fan, too. I was starting to like him more and more. More importantly, I respected him.

After several hours, I saw a man coming toward the building entrance. Right away, I knew it was Guapo. He moved with the confident arrogance of someone who'd been mixed up in gang life for almost 20 years, but was still free to walk the streets. In the upside-down world of street gangs, this made him quite the overachiever.

Tim and I bounced to our feet. He took his place on one side of the doorway. Tim would be the one Guapo saw first. I'd stay near the window, on the opposite side of the door, making sure Guapo had nowhere to run. We heard the door slam shut downstairs and then footsteps leading up toward us. Neither of us had our guns drawn, as there was no reason for that—yet.

The footsteps drew closer. Then Guapo came through the doorway, noticing Tim right away. For a moment, he just walked toward his apartment, showing no signs of being worried.

When Guapo was about 5 feet away, he looked at Tim and spoke harshly. "What's up?" he asked.

Tim showed his badge. "FBI. We'd like to ask you some questions about Julio Valdez."

"Okay," Guapo said, acting cool and calm. Then, a moment later, he pushed Tim backwards. Tim hit the ground hard. Guapo turned around and started off in the other direction, back toward the stairs. I was standing there waiting for him. He looked right at me. Without hesitating, he put his head and huge shoulders down like a linebacker. He was planning to run through me, or over me, whichever was going to get him out of the building. With momentum behind him, and about 50 pounds on me, I wouldn't be able to stop him. There was no time to pull my gun on him either.

When Guapo was within a few inches of me, I side-stepped him. Then I pushed him in the back in the same direction he was already going. I was using the "steam pipe" move that I'd learned at the Academy. It worked perfectly. My push caused Guapo to lose his balance and fall hard to the ground.

Tim rushed over to him and put a knee into his back. I pulled my gun and aimed it at Guapo. "Hands behind your head. Don't move," I said.

"You know what's great about what just happened?" Tim asked. Then he leaned down toward Guapo's ear. "We don't have to ask you to come in for questioning voluntarily anymore." Guapo had just tried to assault a federal agent, a felony for which we could bring him in.

I picked Guapo up by the back of his shirt and we led him toward his apartment. There was no need for a search warrant now. Guapo's trying to run away was more than enough cause to search his property. Tim started turning the place upside down. I stood near Guapo, making sure he didn't make a run for it again.

"I know you," Guapo said, sitting handcuffed to a chair.

"Is that so?" I asked.

"Yeah," he said. "You were a Tigre. You just disappeared."

I nodded. "Best move I ever made," I said. "Whatever happened to Montezuma?"

"Why do you care? He got locked up 'cause of you," Guapo hissed.

I shrugged. "Just curious."

Tim walked out of the bedroom smiling. He was holding a .45-caliber handgun and a large Ziploc filled with white powder. "Look at this, Cortez. A gun and some drugs," he said. "Must be our lucky day."

I put the file containing the crime scene photos on the table in front of Guapo, but didn't reveal any of them yet. "You know why we're here?" I asked.

"Lawyer," Guapo said. "I ain't saying nothin' to you without a lawyer."

I shook my head. "You don't want to do that."

"I would suggest you start talking soon," Tim said, as he slid a picture of the crime scene in front of Guapo.

Guapo looked stone-faced at the photo, not giving anything away. "I didn't do nothing. Lawyer," he repeated.

"If you want, we can bring in a lawyer, charge you for the guns, the drugs and the murder of Julio Valdez. Then we can let a trial settle whether you killed the kid or not. Or, you can tell us where to find whoever did this, and maybe some of this goes away."

"You got nothing. Charge me," Guapo said. Guapo had been dealing with the police for years. He knew we weren't there to arrest him for the murder, because we would've done it already.

"How about the guns and the cocaine?" Tim asked. "Should I charge you for those? What's that, Cortez? About 25 years in the state pen?"

"Yeah, I would say 25," I answered.

Guapo smiled coldly. "There's as many Tigres in lockup as on the streets. What do I got to be afraid of?"

"Where can we find Raffy?" I asked.

Guapo laughed. "Not tellin'," he said.

We needed a new tactic. If Guapo wasn't scared of being arrested, it didn't seem like there was much we could do to get him talking.

As we sat in Guapo's living room, the kids who we'd seen playing stickball passed in the hallway. They stared in, hoping for a glimpse. I thought back to my time in the Tigres and the other members of the gang. It was true. The older guys weren't scared of teachers, police, priests or parents, or even of going to prison. The one thing that seemed to matter to a Tigre was how he looked in front of the other Tigres.

I called Tim back over. "Tim, let's just arrest this guy for the drugs and guns. Then, when we find Raffy, we'll charge him with the murder. He probably did it any-way. And then, we'll make it perfectly clear that it was Guapo over here who told us where to find him."

This really got Guapo's attention. In fact, he tried to jump out of his seat and attack me, despite being cuffed to the chair he sat in. "You can't do that! You're cops. You can't make stuff up."

Tim pushed Guapo back down and leaned toward him. "We're not cops. We are the FBI. We can make you look like the biggest rat the Tigres have ever seen. You think prison would be fun then?" Tim asked.

It didn't take long from there. It turned out that Guapo would rather sell out other Tigres—and keep his own image intact—than have anyone think he worked with police. So, we made a deal with Guapo: We'd arrest him for the drugs we'd found and throw the gun charges out. We'd speak privately to whatever judge sentenced him for the crime, asking him or her to go easy with the sentence. This way, Guapo would spend a few years in jail. None of the Tigres would know that he had cut a deal. In return, he'd help us reel in Raffy, who was the murderer after all, he told us.

He also told us that the weapon Tim recovered in the apartment was the one used in the murder at the Sky-point Theater. Raffy's prints were probably all over it. This would be enough to convict him, but we needed to catch him first.

Guapo revealed that Raffy only spoke on the phone using a burner, a temporary cell phone. He replaced his phone regularly to make sure no one was listening in on his conversations.

"So what do you do when you want to get in touch

with him?" I asked.

"I don't. He calls us," Guapo said. "That's why we call him the ghost."

"How often does he call you?" I asked.

"Pretty much every day," Guapo said.

"Give me your phone," Tim said.

CHAPTER TWELVE

TECHNICAL DIFFICULTIES

We put Guapo into a holding cell at the New York field office. This would keep him out of sight and ensure that he couldn't warn Raffy that we were on to him. Guapo gave us his cell phone and showed us the last number Raffy called him from.

We turned in the gun we found in Guapo's apartment for cataloging and analysis. If Guapo was telling the truth and this was the murder weapon, then Raffy's fingerprints would be enough evidence to put him away for murder.

The next morning, Tim and I took the elevator up to the FBI Laboratory Services office. This is where all of the high-tech stuff happens—the place where they could take a kidnapping victim's picture and add 20 years to see what the victim might look like decades after the crime. It was also the place where a tiny hair or fabric fiber might be analyzed as part of solving a major crime.

There were 15 agents busy at workstations through-out the room. Some worked with test tubes and others at computer monitors. Right away, I spotted the beautiful blond woman I had seen earlier in the day.

"We have to check in with Saunders," Tim said.

"Sounds good to me," I said.

When we reached her, she looked up and smiled at Tim. "Agent O'Rourke, what can I do for you today?" she asked, squeezing the life out of a stress ball.

"Keira Saunders, this is my new partner, Bobby Cortez," Tim said.

I extended my hand to shake hers. I think she forgot that she wasn't still squeezing the stress ball. Her grip was so strong it felt like she was going to break my hand.

"Nice to meet you," I said, jerking my hand backward.

"Sorry," she said. "My doctor said this would help relieve stress. I think maybe I'm overdoing it."

"You're good," I said, not sure what exactly I meant by that.

"Agent Saunders here is the office overachiever—and stress case. Three advanced degrees … and she always gets the bad guy."

"New to the Bureau?" she asked.

I nodded my head "yes."

"Wow, and they put you with this guy?" she said, pointing at Tim. "Heard that his grandfathers and father were cops yet?"

I nodded. "A thousand times."

"So, what's up guys?" Agent Saunders asked.

Tim handed her Guapo's cell phone. "Can you run a trace on the third number in the incoming calls list? We're trying to find out where the call was made from. We're hoping it'll get us a lead on finding the head of the Tigres gang."

"Yup, you got it," Keira said as she started to scroll through the numbers on Guapo's phone. "Give me about 20 minutes. Was the call made from a burner?"

"Probably," I said, smiling like a goofy kid.

"Then we better hope he didn't ditch the phone already," Keira said.

"C'mon, Cortez, we'll come back in 20," Tim said, but I was fascinated by what Keira was working on—and, well, by Keira herself.

"Tim, I'm going to stay and watch Agent Saunders work her magic if it's all right with her," I said.

Tim rolled his eyes. "I'm gonna go get some coffee."

Over the next 20 minutes, I looked on as Keira worked to contact the phone company. Then she accessed a confidential FBI program for tracking cellular phone activity. It was really cool stuff.

Tim returned shortly before she was done. When she was finished, Agent Saunders informed us that Raffy had already disconnected the phone he'd used to call Guapo. There was no way to trace the last call he'd received.

"You're going to have to wait until this Raffy guy calls your contact in the holding cell again," Keira said. "I'll set up a trace on incoming calls to this number. We can see the location of every call this phone receives. Once you confirm that the caller is your guy, I'll be able to tell you where he's calling from."

"Raffy's gotta call him at some point," Tim said. "We'll just hold Guapo until then."

"Wait," I said. "If Guapo just disappears, the first thing they'll think is that he got killed or arrested—especially someone as cautious as Raffy. He's not going to just call him if he hears Guapo hasn't been around."

"That's not a bad point, Rook," Tim said. "Wait, are you saying what I think you're saying? You want to let him go?"

"Keira, can you trace the location of calls to that phone even if you don't have the phone itself?" I asked.

"Sure, I can just put a trace up on the number. As soon as a call comes in, I can get us a location," Keira said. "You'll just need to know which call is the right call—so you don't bust into this guy's grandmother's house or something."

Tim wasn't quite convinced. "Are you suggesting we let one of the most dangerous gangbangers in the city walk out of here? Just hoping he gets a phone call from the leader of the Tigres?"

"And hoping he's doesn't tip his buddies off first," Keira noted.

"I think that's our only shot," I said.

The next morning, Tim and I sat in his car, with Guapo in the backseat. We were two blocks away from Bayline Park.

"You ready?" Tim asked.

Guapo looked nervous.

"You can't go out there looking rattled," Tim said. "Just remember what we told you."

Guapo nodded.

I looked right into his eyes as I spoke to him. "If you ditch your phone, or disappear for any reason, all the Tigres will know about everything you've told us. And you'll get no protection from the FBI. Got it?"

Guapo nodded again.

"You sure we can't put a wire on you?" I asked. "Then we can make sure you're safe."

"Can we just do this?" Guapo asked.

The plan was for Guapo to signal us when he got his daily call from Raffy, by turning his baseball cap around. Then we'd sweep through the park, pick him up along with the other Tigres, and charge him for the drugs we found in his apartment.

As Guapo walked away, Tim and I slowly trailed

behind. We found a parking spot with a good view. We weren't sure how long we'd be waiting. After all, Raffy might not call him for hours, or he might not call at all. We used FBI-issued binoculars to watch Guapo from about 200 yards away.

Guapo walked right up to a group of Tigres. The younger Tigres all greeted him warmly. Two older Tigres walked up to him next. One of them was much taller than Guapo. The other was about his size, but wiry, and wearing a familiar-looking jacket. After a moment, I realized that I was looking at the guy in the hoodie that I'd chased along the rooftops. He put his arm around Guapo and they started walking off together. It looked like a friendly discussion.

All of a sudden, the large Tigre grabbed Guapo by the collar of his T-shirt and clocked him across the cheek. As Guapo fell to the ground, both Tigres started kicking him.

We both put down our binoculars and hurried out of the car. Tim got on his radio right away. "Backup needed at Bayline Park. Hurry!" I saw the same young Tigres who had just greeted Guapo so warmly now kicking and punching him on the ground.

I ran a few steps ahead of Tim toward the fight, but they were deep inside the park. As we ran toward them, the kid I'd chased on the rooftops started waving the group to stand back. I watched him pull out a gun. We were getting closer, but weren't there yet. The kid in the hoodie aimed his gun toward Guapo.

Then I heard a gunshot come from behind me. I looked back and saw Tim firing his gun in the air. This got the attention of the Tigres, who hadn't seen us until then.

"Freeze," I screamed, pulling out my gun. "FBI!"

Suddenly, the kid in the hoodie aimed his gun in our direction. A stream of bullets whizzed by. I took cover behind a tree until the shots had stopped. By then, the entire gang had begun to scatter in different directions. I ran as fast as I could toward Guapo.

When I reached him, I found him badly beaten, but alive.

"They knew," Guapo said, grimacing in pain. "Someone must've seen me talking to you. Might as well kill me, Cortez—I'm already dead."

We hadn't exactly been sneaky when we went to see Guapo. I remembered that the kids playing stickball had walked by. It could've been them, or any neighbor of Guapo's, that had seen us yesterday. They obviously let the Tigres know about our little visit.

Guapo was no longer of any use to us. Catching Raffy was going to be even harder. We were going to have to explain to McDowell that our lead had gone cold, that Raffy was still on the loose, and that the Tigres were as ferocious as ever.

CHAPTER THIRTEEN

COLD CASE

Our drive back to the field office was quiet. Tim and I knew we'd taken a risk and it hadn't worked out. We'd still be able to arrest Guapo after he received medical care. But now we'd have to make sure he was protected from the Tigres. That would be close to impossible. Any prison sentence he received would likely turn into a death sentence at the hands of his former gang mates.

Raffy, "the ghost" who had likely killed the man in the Skypoint Theater, was still far from our grasp. He was running the Tigres from a distance. It felt like we'd made zero progress. Director McDowell was not going to be very happy with us.

On our way up to the director's office, I apologized to Tim for how badly my plan had turned out. "We're partners," he replied. "No matter how things turn out in the field, it's nobody's fault once it's over."

Sitting across from McDowell a little later, Tim and

I went through everything that had happened.

"This was your plan, Cortez?" McDowell asked.

"Well, sir. I thought—"

Tim cut me off. "We came up with the plan together, sir."

Although he wasn't happy about it, McDowell was more understanding than I expected. I knew that part of this understanding was due to his respect for Tim.

"Gentlemen, I hate to say this, but there doesn't seem to be anything else you can move on," McDowell said. "So I've got to reassign you two to some other cases. Then I've got to start a formal investigation, which means coordinating with NYPD, and—"

"A lot of red tape that's going to undo all the progress we made this week," Tim said in a frustrated tone.

"We can't just walk away, sir!" I said. "We're getting closer. If we can bring in Raffy, we can shut these guys down, permanently."

"Patience," McDowell said. "You'll get your chance at these guys again. But right now, I need you two on some other things."

"But, sir. . ." I said, not ready to give up.

"Dismissed, gentlemen," McDowell said.

On our way out of McDowell's office, Agent Saunders raced down the hall toward us. She was holding a piece of paper. "Agent Cortez," she said, "this email just came in for you."

I read the email and then handed it to Tim.

"What's going on?" McDowell asked, poking his head out of his office.

Tim finished reading and answered, "Sir, I think we have something that might change your mind."

"Is that so?" McDowell asked curiously.

Tim handed McDowell the piece of paper:

FROM: 1140595114@gmail.com
TO: LabServices@FBI.NY.gov
SUBJECT: Raffy
To Bobby Cortez,

Too much heat on the street in Skypoint for Raffy. Get him here: Obelisk, Central Park, 10 PM

—You're Welcome (again)

It was another anonymous tip, just like the first one I'd received—the one that started this whole thing. This tip seemed to have come from the same person, although he had changed his email address.

"Where do these tips keep coming from?" Tim asked.

I shrugged. I wished I knew.

"You sure have luck on your side, Cortez. This is your last chance, gentlemen," McDowell said. "Bring him in tonight."

After McDowell dismissed the three of us, Keira followed us down the hall and into the elevator. "I'm coming with you guys," she said. "I'm totally into this case, and you guys are going to need the extra hands. No arguing."

"Welcome to the team," I said.

The three of us arrived in Manhattan at the East 81st Street entrance to Central Park at about 8 p.m. We couldn't risk bringing backup to the stakeout and scaring Raffy off. We were wearing bulletproof vests under our clothes.

According to the email tip, Raffy would be at the famous Obelisk structure in two hours. The Obelisk looked like a smaller version of the famous Washington Monument in Washington, D.C.

We found a place to hide while we kept an eye on the area around the Obelisk. We used night vision binocular goggles, so we could monitor the area from about 200 yards away.

We waited, passing the time by telling jokes and sharing stories. Finally, the clock approached 10 o'clock. We saw a group of five Tigres walk into the area near the Obelisk. They were overly cautious and a few of them looked to be armed. None of them was Raffy, though. Shortly afterward, another four Tigres walked up and starting talking with the group that was already there.

Then two more Tigres walked up. I could tell that

one of them was my old friend. My heart raced at the sight of him. He looked almost exactly the same. The guy he came with was a huge figure about twice Raffy's size. Guapo had mentioned to us that, paranoid as ever, Raffy employed a full-time bodyguard.

We waited another minute as the group of thugs made their way over to Raffy. The Tigre drug business had grown in recent years. These kids, who came from families with very little money, gave Raffy credit for putting money in their pockets. When you struggled like they did, it was hard to see everything that was wrong with selling drugs and committing crimes.

"Let's move," Tim said.

The three of us sneakily approached, moving from behind one tree to another. We got within 100 yards and could see the group more clearly. There wasn't much to hide behind the rest of the way, aside from the cover of night. We knew we'd have to move quickly, hoping the Tigres wouldn't see us until we were right on them.

On Tim's signal, we began a full-on sprint toward the group. Our guns were drawn and we were ready for whatever happened next. We reached the group of Tigres pretty quickly. Unfortunately, when we were about 50 yards away, one of them spotted us. "Cops!" he yelled.

Then, all hell broke loose. Several of the Tigres drew guns and fired toward us. Raffy pulled his gun out as well, firing three times. I heard one of the bullets whiz right past me. Raffy then sprinted off with his bodyguard. The two of them headed onto a path leading to one of the large stone bridges in the park.

I headed after Raffy. Looking over my shoulder, I expected to see Tim and Keira following. When I turned, though, I saw that each of them was now fighting with a Tigre.

I considered going back to help. Then I noticed two more police cars racing toward the park in the distance, obviously responding to the sound of shots being fired. Tim looked up at me as he slapped handcuffs onto a Tigre. He yelled, "Don't let him get away!"

I knew I was on my own for the moment—prepared for a showdown with my old friend. My night vision goggles were slowing me down, so I tossed them aside. The bad news was that when I reached a tunnel up ahead, I couldn't see inside. I had no idea what to expect.

I carefully started making my way through, unable to see anything for a few moments. I sped up my pace as I reached a streak of light at the end of the tunnel. The moment I felt the fresh air hit my face, it felt like I had run into a brick wall. Actually, it was a fist. I found myself flat on my back, looking up at the bodyguard Raffy had brought with him. A few steps behind him, I saw Raffy.

My gun had flown from my hand when the big man hit me. I tried to roll toward my gun, but the bodyguard pushed me back to the ground. I punched his knee as hard as I could, which temporarily got him off my chest. But by then, Raffy had picked up my gun and pointed it at me.

Once Raffy had my own gun trained on me, the bodyguard stepped back. Raffy recognized me right away. "Bobby Cortez, what a twist," he said. "You know, I heard you were a cop now, but I really had to see it myself to believe it. What a punk!" he shouted. He pointed the gun so it was touching my right cheek. I looked into his eyes. It was obvious that the Raffy I knew was long gone.

He continued, "I'd ask you how you were doing after all these years. But it's obvious that you're not doing so well at the moment, huh?"

Raffy still had the same know-it-all tone he'd had when he was the smartest kid in our school.

"Raffy—" I started.

"It's Espectro!" he said angrily. "Have some respect! Raffy was a punk. He got picked on all the time after his two best friends ran out on him. Raffy was afraid of his own shadow. After you left, the Tigres took me in and taught me how to be a man. Then I taught them how to run a city! I own Skypoint, Cortez."

"No you don't, Raffy," I said.

He walked over and kicked me in the stomach. "That's for trying to get Guapo to give me up," Raffy said. Then he kicked me again. "And that's for never even calling up your homeboys and tellin' them where you went." He kicked me again, this time directly in my face. "And that's for coming back here like you still count—'cause you don't!"

I spit blood onto the ground, wincing in pain. "You think this is being a man? Bossing around a bunch of teenagers and hiding in the shadows?"

"Better than being a pig," he said. "And, I bet I got more money in my pocket right now than you got in your bank account."

"Raffy, it doesn't have to be like this," I said.

"Call me Espectro! Raffy is dead. And you will be soon, too!" He grabbed me by the hair and turned me around so my back was to him. Then he lifted the safety on his gun with a click.

"Don't do this," I said.

"Say goodbye, Cortez," he said.

I closed my eyes, regretting that I'd never get a chance to say goodbye to my father. I waited to hear the final bang of the gun. Instead, I heard a scuffle break out behind me.

I turned around and saw Raffy fighting with a large man in a red jacket. The darkness made it impossible to see who he was. I got up and cut off Raffy's bodyguard before he could help him. Then I threw a left hook in the bodyguard's cheek and stunned him for a second.

Raffy was scuffling on the ground with the man in the red jacket. My gun was lying a few feet away from them. The bodyguard saw it too, but I reached the gun first and pointed it back at him. He ran off, but I wasn't about to chase after him—not with Raffy in my sights.

Now, I pointed my gun at Raffy and the stranger in the red jacket. "Freeze," I said, "both of you."

The stranger backed away from Raffy, and then Raffy tried reaching into his pocket. I could barely see in the darkness, but it looked like he was going for his own gun.

"Freeze!" I repeated. "Don't think I won't shoot you, Raffy!"

Raffy put his hands in the air, just as Tim came running up to us.

"You all right?" I asked him.

"Most of 'em ran away. We've got a couple of unis back there now with Agent Saunders rounding up the ones we caught. You okay?"

I gestured over toward Raffy, still aiming my gun at him. "He's got a gun. Grab it and cuff him, would you?" I asked.

Tim walked over and grabbed the gun out of his jacket. He slapped handcuffs on Raffy, reading him his rights and arresting him for murder.

"What about this guy?" Tim asked, pointing at the man in the red jacket. I had barely looked in his direction until now. When I did, I recognized his face immediately. "Jorge?" I asked, totally confused. I hadn't seen him since the day he stole that money—with my help—from

Mamacita's bodega.

"You didn't have an FBI email address yet," Jorge said, putting his hands down and smiling. "So I just sent messages to the email address on the website. I hoped my tips got to you."

I walked up to him and gave my old friend a bear hug. "You saved my life," I said. "You're a hero, man."

"That's what you do for old friends," Jorge said. "Besides, you saved my life a long time ago. When you left, it really turned me around."

"How'd you know I was back in the city, and in the FBI?" I asked.

"My uncle is friendly with a few guys who know your dad. He tells everybody about you. The old man is proud of you, we all are," he said. "I would have called you. But I didn't know if you'd still be mad after everything that happened when we were kids."

"No, man," I said, giving him another hug. "We all change."

As we walked out of the park, with Raffy in hand-cuffs, I asked Jorge, "How'd you know where Raffy would be?"

It turned out that Jorge was now running the community center down on East 94th Street. He was helping to keep kids out of trouble. He told me about how the Tigres had made the neighborhood worse and worse in recent years. Since Raffy became the leader, there were more drugs on the street than ever. "Some of the Tigres use the computers at the center for email," he said. "When the drugs and murders started piling up in Skypoint, I started hacking into their email accounts. I find leads and pass them along to the police whenever I can."

Tim went up ahead to help Agent Saunders and the unis. I led a handcuffed Raffy toward our car with Jorge on the other side of me. For a brief moment, the three of us walked side by side—just like we had so many years ago. None of us said a word about the strangeness of the moment. Still, I knew we were all thinking about it.

I loaded Raffy into the back of Tim's car and said goodbye to Jorge. "Let's get together. We can grab a slice at Mario's," I said, still hassling him about the best pizza in Brooklyn.

"Or we can go to Original's and get some real pizza," he replied.

"Next time you've got a tip, no need to deliver it anonymously. Any time you hear about heat on the street, let me know."

We shook hands and Jorge made his way back to Skypoint, which was a little safer than before, for the moment at least.

Tim and Keira headed back to the field office to book Raffy and charge him with murder. I headed home for a long, deep sleep.

CHAPTER FOURTEEN

REFUND

A few days later, I received my first paycheck from the FBI. I knew what I had to do with it—part of it at least.

I had planned to visit my father for the weekend in Buffalo. He lived alone, so I tried to visit as much as I could. On the way up, I'd arranged to pick up his old friend, Patrice. She was finishing her last week of work at the 138th Precinct in Brooklyn. She was about to retire after being a cop for almost 30 years. Like Dad, she was still single. Even though she and my dad hadn't spoken in years, he talked about her all the time.

I dropped by the 138th Precinct, and Patrice confessed that she still thought about my father all the time. It took a few minutes, but I finally convinced her to head up to Buffalo with me for the weekend to surprise my dad.

On my way out of Skypoint, I wanted to make one more stop. I drove down Avenue L, to Mamacita's bodega. I hadn't been in there since the day Jorge and I had stolen from them so many years before.

Mamacita wasn't there, but her son Alfred was still faithfully working in the store. He was in the back, stocking shelves, when I walked in. "Do you have an ATM?" I called to the back.

Alfred looked at me, but showed no sign of recognition so many years later. "On your left," he yelled.

I took out some cash from the ATM and grabbed a Yoo-hoo. Alfred turned away from the shelf he was stocking for a moment. "Just the Yoo-hoo?" he asked.

I nodded.

"Two bucks," he said. "You can leave it on the counter."

I put two dollars down, then reached into my pocket and took out the cash from the ATM. I counted out $320 and put that down, too. "Have a nice day," I said.

"You too," he called out, without looking up at me. I was thrilled to have a chance to return the money we'd stolen so many years before. I hustled out of Mamacita's, hopped in my car and pulled away. Through the rearview I saw Alfred Aguilera race out of the store, holding the money I'd left and yelling after me, "You forgot your money!" I smiled, watching Alfred get smaller and smaller in my mirror as I drove down Avenue L. For the first time, I felt like I could truly leave my past behind, and drive into the future.

Test Yourself ... Are You a Professional Reader?

Chapter 1

1. Who is Tim O'Rourke?

2. The main character, Bobby Cortez, is a young FBI agent, but he didn't take the typical path to get there. What did he do before he became an FBI agent?

3. Tim and Bobby discover a body in the Skypoint Theater. How did they know to go there?

Essay:

Tim likes to do everything "by the book," but Bobby likes to do things his own way. What is good about doing something your own way, and what is bad about it? When do you do things your own way, and when do you do them by the book?

Chapter 2

1. Why did Tim not tell the director that Bobby had run after the suspect by himself?

2. Who are the Tigres?

3. Why does McDowell want Bobby to work on this case?

Essay:

Bobby wants to be an FBI agent to help protect kids from gangs. If you were an FBI agent, what would you want to do, and why?

Chapter 3

1. Who are Jorge and Raffy, and what are they like?

2. Bobby, Jorge and Raffy don't have enough money to ride the Cyclone. What is Bobby's plan?

3. Chapter 3 ends with the line: "Unfortunately, nothing ever stays the same." What does this mean? Why does the chapter end this way?

Essay:

Who are your best friends? What do you do together? Do you do different things with different people?

Chapter 4

1. Now that Bobby and his friends are freshmen in high school, what has changed? Why is hanging out on the "L," the street where gangs often hang out, different for them?

2. What does Jorge want Bobby to do that Bobby doesn't want to do? Why does Jorge want to do this?

3. How do the three friends escape from Alfred when he is chasing them?

Essay:

What is happening between Raffy and Jorge? Are they still friends? What has changed?

Chapter 5

1. What is "The Crib," and why does Jorge take Bobby there?

2. How does Bobby feel when they are inside The Crib? What does he think about the Tigres?

3. Why is Bobby surprised when Jorge shows Guapo the cash he stole from Mamacita's?

Essay:

Why do you think kids like Bobby want to be in gangs? What makes it seem cool? What are the downsides?

Chapter 6

1. Who is Officer Kenyon? Why does Bobby think she is at his house? Why is she really there?

2. According to Guapo, what is the reason that Bobby was not arrested for helping Jorge steal from Mamacita's?

3. What do the Tigres want from Bobby?

Essay:

In chapter 6, Bobby was initiated into the Tigres. What kind of things are the Tigres going to expect from him? What groups are you a member of? What kind of things are expected of you by that group?

Chapter 7

1. The title of chapter 7 is "Two Bobbys." What does this mean? Who are the two Bobbys?

2. Why does Raffy say that he doesn't want Bobby to hang out with him anymore?

3. What happens between Bobby and his dad when they go to the Mets game? What do they talk about?

Essay:

Bobby feels bad for keeping things from his dad. Have you or has anyone you know ever kept something from a parent? What was it? How did you/they feel and what happened?

Chapter 8

1. How does Bobby feel about the upcoming fight with the Aviadors?

2. What does Bobby realize as he and the Tigres are walking toward the place where they are going to meet the Aviadors for the fight?

3. What does Bobby decide to do?

Essay:

Question: Bobby decides that his dreams of college and track are more important than being in the gang. What dreams and goals do you have? How important are they to you?

Chapter 9

1. How is Bobby's life in Buffalo different from his life in Brooklyn?

2. What is Hogan's Alley?

3. What are two subjects FBI agents have to be trained in?

Essay:

Bobby says that it felt very different being initiated into the FBI than it did when he was initiated into the Tigres. In what ways do you think he felt differently? Why do you think he felt this way?

Chapter 10

1. Why do you think Bobby felt like being an FBI agent was what he "was always meant to do"?

2. What was important about the rubber bands that Bobby pointed out at the crime scene?

3. What do Bobby and Tim think was the reason for the murder? Why do they think someone painted "Mordida Feroz" on the wall?

Essay:

What do you think of their detective work? Does it sound like a logical explanation for the crime? In what ways does the evidence support or refute their conclusion? What other possible explanations can you think of?

Chapter 11

1. When people bought drugs from the Tigres, they had to pay their money to the dealer and then get a beeper number. Then, someone would call them to arrange a delivery. Why did they have this system?

2. Why does Tim want to follow the Tigre for a couple of blocks before they pick him up?

3. What is Raffy's nickname, and why do they call him that?

Essay:

Bobby grew up in Skypoint, surrounded by gangs, while Tim

grew up in the suburbs. What kind of area did you grow up in, and how has it influenced you and your views on the world?

Chapter 12

1. Why do they decide to let Guapo go?

2. How did the gang members know that Guapo had talked to the police?

3. At the end of chapter 12, Guapo gets picked up by an ambulance and Bobby and Tim are left in the park to think about their situation. How has their situation changed since the beginning of the chapter? Is it better or worse?

Essay:
Who is your favorite character? Why?

Chapter 13

1. How did McDowell react when Tim and Bobby told him about how badly their plan had worked out?

2. What happens to put Tim and Bobby back on Raffy's trail?

3. Where does Bobby catch up to Raffy?

Essay:
Were you surprised that Jorge was the one sending Bobby the anonymous tips? Why or why not? What other books and movies do you know that have twist endings?

Chapter 14

1. What does Bobby do with his first paycheck from the FBI?

2. Who does Bobby bring to visit his dad?

3. At the end, Bobby says he feels like he could truly leave his past behind him. Why does he feel like this?

Essay:
What will you do with your first paycheck? Why?